AF415070

Don't Be A Dumb Bitch

Ayana Ellis

Published by Ayana Ellis, 2015.

This is a work of fiction. Similarities to real people, places, or events are entirely coincidental.

DON'T BE A DUMB BITCH

First edition. May 24, 2015.

Copyright © 2015 Ayana Ellis.

ISBN: 979-8224406746

Written by Ayana Ellis.

I am not a relationship expert. There is no fame or big name behind this. This book is written by a female from Brooklyn who graduated from the School of Hard Knocks, and I just want to share what I've learned, experienced, seen, and heard with you all. I can't give you my point of view about what men should do because I am not one. I can only speak from a woman's point of view on the things that we do and allow to happen to us and how we can possibly change our ways to obtain a happier, healthier life. This is not a book about pointing the finger and belittling the less knowledgeable. In order to write this book, I too had to have made some not so smart decisions in my life. This is real, straight up, round table talk with my readers about love, life, and relationships.

First, allow me to explain the meaning behind the title of this book. I am in no way degrading our women or contributing to the disrespect that we have to endure on the day to day. We deal with enough misogyny as is and though my words may come off raw, my message is very clear. I want women to win! I want us to love ourselves more, love one another more, love our friends more, and not put so much emphasis on wanting a man, needing a man, trying to impress a man or being so desperate for love and acceptance that we settle for half of a man. I've done some research to put this book together and through my studies I have found that men simply aren't courting us anymore because we aren't courting ourselves. If we act like basic "bitches," then that's how we will be treated. However, I've also found that you men aren't worth much of a damn either especially those of you claiming that "Hos are winning." The way I see it, neither sex has any room to judge the other. We have to come to the understanding and realization that we should not be at war with one another. We are supposed to be learning from and loving one another.

The way that we are exploited on television is not helping us at all either. Just like so many of us who have lost our way, so have these women on television. They are from where we are from and they are lashing out while looking for love like the rest of us. The issue is, you have young girls sitting at home viewing these women on television as celebrities and role models, and there goes the neighborhood. They don't realize that the pain is just being glamorized.

Another problem is, we aren't dealing with the kind of men that our grandmothers married. The head of the household is too busy chasing a rap career. Where have our men gone? And let me be clear, when I say ni**a, I'm not addressing just black men, I'm addressing all men. Sure, as women, we have to fend for ourselves and make sure that we have all of the resources to care for ourselves, etc., but where are our men? What have they done for us lately?

In summation, there is no book that can tell a person how to get a man, how to live, what to do, how to be happy, etc. As individuals, we know what we want and what is best for us. We know that the answer is right inside of us, waiting at our core for us to dig deep enough to reach it. Nobody else has the map to your happiness but you. However, we all could use some inspiration to get going. As an author, what I can do is share these chapters and scenarios in hopes that one person can relate and make a change for the better. There is something in here for everybody to relate to. Whether you are a single mother trying to juggle dating, an ex-wife or baby mama trying to move on, a career woman struggling to find time for her relationship, a woman wanting to hold on to her love, or a female with no attachments that simply wants to be happy, I try my best to provide you with advice. Keep in mind that I can't give my opinions to you the way Steve Harvey did or how Iyanla Vanzant has done, but it is my goal, just like others before me, to inspire and enlighten you... my way, the street but sweet way. I can only hope you can receive and respect that.

There's rules to this shit... I wrote me a manual.

Gem

"The greatest gift a woman can give to her kids is loving and respecting herself. The love you give yourself today, will affect the life you give tomorrow."

IF YOU SMOKE CRACK TODAY...YOUR KIDS WILL SMOKE CRACK TOMORROW

We like who we like, whether he is good or bad for us. We go through ups and downs and put ourselves through avoidable situations because we believe that we are strong enough to handle the consequences and the addiction of drama. I'm sure every crack addict felt the same way. I won't get addicted. I'm stronger than the rest of these fiends. Years later, you find yourself jobless, missing teeth, addicted to drugs, and fucked up in the game just because you put yourself in a situation that you knew you shouldn't have. That's cool provided that the only person that you are responsible for is you. But when you have children, the game automatically changes. When your little man or princess is old enough to talk and point, that is the time when you need to stop dating men that have nothing to offer your children. Most importantly, stop dating these men that have nothing to offer you! I get that, when your heart is broken you go through that, I don't give a fuck phase, which causes us to date recklessly, inadvertently doing the same thing to your child that the father is doing or has done It's your job as a woman to build positive, long-lasting, healthy relationships for your kid, but, first, you have to create a long- lasting, loving relationship with yourself. You have to heal and stop victimizing yourself as a single mother. Woe-is-me cannot work when you're raising children. I know it's hard, but it will and can get better, but you have to be willing to put in that work. You can't just give up on yourself and bring just any man around just to have a warm body in your bed. Your children deserve to see you in a better situation than a mediocre one. Now, I know there are a few women reading this and saying, "Well, my man has a good job. He does this for me and that for me," but see, the thing is this, if this man doesn't see anything wrong with you spending all of your time with him, instead of your kids, then, guess what? He is not a good man! What kind of man respects or would allow a woman that he really cares about to neglect her children? What kind of man would be comfortable with a woman who would rather be up under him cooking and catering but doesn't treat her children with that same love and attention? Do keep in mind that you are raising someone's wife, husband, father, or mother. The child you're rearing will grow up to be something to someone. What will that something be? How will they treat people, and how will they allow themselves to be treated?

The family structure, especially in African American homes, is damn near extinct. A lot of men that date single mothers aren't really trying to be a replacement father. You can't even trust these men around your children, with all of this rape and molestation going on, so why are you so careless with your precious cargo? Though the children aren't saying anything, they are indeed watching. A child may not be able to articulate what it is they see or feel, but they will show us exactly where we failed as parents by their actions when they get older. Once you become a parent, there is no such thing as mama/daddy gotta have a life, too. Your kids are your life, and you need to date for them. So what if their father is in their lives? The men you date can still influence them. You had your time to fuck up, so don't fuck up their innocent lives by bringing the ain't-shit men around and then, on top of that, neglecting them. Get it right for them because there is nothing sadder than a child that feels unloved. Little girls will search for that love high and low. She will search for that love under men, in drugs, in alcohol, and by any means necessary. That young girl will get her fix of love if you don't give it to her. You do not want your son out in the streets robbing folks, hustling, or joining gangs and shit to get the love that he should have gotten at home. You don't want your daughter out prostituting, hanging out, and dressing like a THOT (hood translation: that ho over there) to get attention because mommy is too busy being selfish. These men will be there waiting with bated breath for you to make time for them. As your children are growing, you have to focus on raising them. They deserve to look back on their childhood and remember being loved and paid attention to by their parents. Remember, you were a child once. What are some of the things you wish your parents would have done differently? Be the change that you wanted to see... then.

Gem

"The key to getting everything you want from a man is to need nothing from him at all."

GOALDIGGERS VS GOLDDIGGERS

In the words of Kanye, 'No one man should have all that power.' It's sad to say ladies that we give men the power by lowering our standards for a handbag, some shoes or a vacation. Most women blame this behavior on the fact that "men ain't shit," so they're just going to get a man for all that he's got. We complain that all men want is pussy. Well let me ask you this—why should a man risk giving you his heart when you show him that all you really want from him is a pair of shoes and a bag to match? You may perceive it as all men want is pussy. Maybe that's all you have to offer, and you didn't even realize it. Or maybe you do realize it, and you're okay with it. A man knows exactly what it is he's doing to bait the kind of female he wants, and the kind of female he can flaunt. Whose fault is it that a man can approach us with the mere image of having money and we instantly start grinning up in his face without really knowing shit about him except for what we see? And how do you expect him to treat you, knowing that you're only attracted to him and going so hard to keep his attention because he has or appears to have money?

When was the last time you were in or even around someone in a healthy relationship that could give you a sense of hope? Now I'm not talking about some cat that you were dealing with that used to take you out, come through and hit and sit on your couch for a few hours. I can bet my bottom dollar that if there was someone in a healthy relationship around you, you stopped hanging around them because their happiness annoyed you. You didn't stick around your happy friend or acquaintance to see how a good man treats his woman or what happiness looks like. You choose not to see the good in relationships because you're so used to losing. So you decide that you're going to use men for money and blame your behavior on how men act. Now how ass backwards is that? How can someone else's behavior determine how you treat yourself and what you allow? Okay, so now you're on this mission to get you a baller, aka a man that has enough money to trick on any chick and make any simple-minded woman feel special by dropping a few grand on absolutely nothing. Nothing, meaning you, not the bags and shoes and trips, but you. Now I'm not trying to insult you, sweetie. I'm just telling you what it is.

Let me ask you ladies: What ever happened to the regular guys? You know, the man with the job, the 401k, that steady paycheck that comes home every day? Is that not enough anymore? Everybody has to be a baller? Are we so fiend out to live the "good life" that we will trade in our souls to lay up with a man that can give two shits about us, as long as we look good at his expense? Are we too desperate and lazy to get our own? But then you have the nerve to complain about men and their doggish ways. How do you think you're acting, young lady? Not to mention, when you lower your standards for a few dollars, you have the nerve to turn the other cheek on him being unfaithful. You swear you sound like you're saying something deep when you say that all men cheat and you don't care as long as you don't catch him. You are already setting yourself up for disrespect when you let a man know he can disrespect your union, just don't get caught. He already knows that he does not have to respect you. He does not have to protect you, and he doesn't have to do anything to show you how much he values you because you don't give a damn about yourself. But you expect him to? It's not okay for your man, your mate, your partner to cheat on you and put your emotions and health at risk because you give him the green light to. If a man makes the decision to be with you, be committed to you, and be a part of your life in such a way, then it is his job to earn his keep by being responsible, faithful, and committed to just you. But why should he if you're telling him it's okay to be community dick, just don't get caught. Imagine, for one second, how disrespected you would feel if your man, the one that is supposed to love and cherish you, tells you that you can go fuck other men just don't get caught. Would you feel respected or loved at all? But you're such a gold digger, knee deep in trying to come up that you don't even realize how much you are failing and how much further you have to go.

Money is a man's power, and, when you take away a man's power, you force him into submission. You strip him of what he values most and then, and only then, will you see what he thinks of you and, most importantly, himself. When a man can hide behind his bank account, he knows that he can have any bitch at his disposal. He doesn't have to give himself to you, which means that his feelings for you will not grow. And you know what that means? It means that you can be easily replaced because he really doesn't give two shits about you. He knows that you're in it for the dough. He's seen your kind before. You are not the first or the last chick he encountered with hungry eyes. When you're a woman that doesn't value the dollar, you force this man to put his cash away and come up with something clever, more creative, and more personal. Now, he has to show you what he can do for you outside of buying you shit and taking you places. But as long as you have a price on your pussy and he knows that all he has to do is toss you a couple of dollars, you have put yourself in the barnyard with the rest of the chickens who think that fucking and sucking will solidify their spot in a man's life and home. You are up against thousands of women that have the same mentality as you. How do you expect to win? Are you even trying to win? Or are you just merely existing and trying to get by? You can't let what a man brings to the table be the only shit you got to eat, come on now.

You have a lot of these women who think they are doing something big when they get small change from these men. There is so much more that a man who really cares about you can offer you outside of material bullshit. Being provided for has nothing to do with the amount of money a man puts in your hands, but everything to do with the amount of time he invests in you. Any fool with money can give a chick a few dollars and any chick that never had shit will be impressed. A man doesn't love you and respect you because he bought you something. You'll know how much you mean to him when he taught you some thing, you know what I'm talking about? When you have a man who wants to bring you into his lifestyle and is willing to share himself with you, as opposed to giving you a tiny percentage, of what he is worth, then you are winning. Any and everything else is child's play, so step your game up, ladies. Command more with your self-respect! Don't strive to be a ho or gold digger. Despite what you heard, hos are not winning, and men do not love them. Men don't love hos. Sometimes, men can be some lazy muthafuckas who don't have what it takes to put in the work it requires to be with a real woman whose character commands respect and fidelity, so they settle for hos until that time comes, and for some men, that's never.

Remember, not too long ago, when men were chivalrous? He opened the car door for us, he catered to us, brought us flowers, took us dancing, wined and dined us, and, when he entered our homes after dating for a certain amount of time, he asked to meet the kids. He started leaving money on the table, and he'd fixed things around the house—all without us having to ask and all without us having to force ourselves on these men. I think what happened was we got lazy, and we dropped our goals and picked up all of these bad habits along the way. We started doing too much to get kept when we don't even have to do all that. Just be a lady, be about your business, respect yourself and it will all fall into place without you having to sacrifice your dignity and while you're taking care of yourself, you should be generating your own income, so you won't have to sell yourself to get small change at someone else's expense. I promise you if you spend more time focused on your goals, practicing becoming a better woman every day, respecting yourself and not selling yourself short just for a quick come up, your life will be so much richer than you could ever imagine. The risks are too high to place your soul in someone else's hands for money and a lifestyle. A woman with her own, aka a Goal Digger doesn't have these kinds of problems. She's secure with her own and her only mission is to keep growing her own empire. She doesn't have to chase a man down for money. She doesn't have to sacrifice herself for a few dollars. All she has to do is be great like she's been, and greatness will come her way. Focus on getting your own throne and stop settling for a rented one.

Gem

"Don't Choose Dick over Your Dignity"

PREDATOR vs PREY

You ever heard someone say that you're not supposed to go food shopping when you're hungry because you'll go to the supermarket and buy all kinds of things that you don't need? The same rules apply for men. Don't go looking for a man when you're lonely and horny. Men can sniff out a horny, lonely, desperate woman a mile away. It doesn't matter how reserved you try to be. It doesn't matter the kind of woman that you claim to be, if you're not living it, it holds no weight. Women suffer from two diseases. One is "Toomuchdickinyaitis" and that is when a woman is just doing too much. You're having sex with different partners and for no real reason other than to fill a void. The other is the opposite of that, it is "Lackadickaphobia." You get no dick and, when you do, you latch on to that it like a newborn on a nipple.

A predator can always tell when a woman is suffering from Lackadickaphobia. We're so thirsty and don't even realize it. We leave food in the microwave and the key under the mat for this dude. We let him hit it whenever he wants to hit it, and we don't ask him for shit in return. Men need you to set some standards, and they need to know that this woman is not going to let him get away with just any kind of behavior. Even if you're lying to yourself, set some standards for this man to follow. But when you are suffering from "Dickmatization," you just forget every damn thing your mama taught you. Dickmatization is very real, but, like most addictions, you can beat this ladies! Never trust some good dick and a smile. Stay strong because some men are always on predator mode, looking for that easy prey, all day. And the hard-working woman with so much on her plate that can't find a date is the first one to get eaten. *Pun Intended*

Most men are always on predator mode, and they can almost always smell desperation on a woman like a dog senses fear. Maintain that deep desire and yearning to have another in your life, or you will be someone's prey, and it won't be pretty. Hungry, lonely pussy and good dick are a recipe for dicksaster. Lord have mercy. You will be outside looking for him in the daytime with a flashlight, a mattress tied to your back, a bullhorn to call his name, and waving your wallet in the air trying to buy that nigga if your ass ain't careful. So whatever you do, do not desperately seek out anyone other than yourself. Don't let loneliness steer you down the wrong road.

Also, ladies, here is our most common mistake, we equate sex with love. No matter how much we think we don't, we do. We love with our pussies and get emotional when dick is involved. It is almost impossible to have a consistent sexual relationship with someone and not catch some kind of feelings. And when we catch these feelings, we begin to feel as if the man is obligated to us once we allow him inside of us, and that's partially true. But it is also a gamble. All because we feel this way doesn't mean that the man will understand it and reciprocate. As adults, I think that we all need to be fucking for a purpose bigger than money, a good time, or to get over someone else. And as women, the older we get the more vulnerable we get. The average fuck is not just an average fuck, no matter how much we try to think that it is. Our needs and wants change as we get older and more mature and with that comes emotion. Our desire and hunger for more will, of course, keep any man coming around for seconds and thirds. We are not men. We are not designed to be like men. We are women, and we are supposed to be okay with being gentle and equating sex with love. We are supposed to limit who we give ourselves to, aren't we? Now, this man is getting some good hungry loving from a woman who wants nothing more than to feel a man's touch and to be loved because she is tired of playing with toys and she needs affection. After all, she works hard and deserves to let her hair down. The sexual chemistry will most likely be phenomenal. But this woman confuses the time that the man spends with her with the emotion of love. She thinks that this man is always around her because he cares about her. Maybe he does begin to care as time goes on, but the relationship isn't built on that. It's built on lust, and there is no relationship in the world that can grow or last on that foundation alone. You have to be real with yourself, ladies, and get it through your head that this man is around you because your body is always calling. He wants that pussy first and foremost, and the moment you try to switch gears, he is outta there. You are now in a situationship. See how that happened? The passion, lust, and chemistry that is created in that bedroom needs to remain right there next to the wet spot. It is what it is, and, because we are so emotional, we refuse to believe that. At what point did love come into the picture? You love the sex, you love the intimacy, you love how he makes you feel physically and sexually, but you have to learn how to separate your love from the sexual aspect of the relationship and face the reality of what it is really about. It's about a hungry person getting fed, and that goes both ways!

You need to stop cummin' from your heart and learn how to cum with just your vagina alone. But we are women, and no matter how tough you believe that you are, you will catch feelings. You cannot just cum from your vagina and not begin to feel something for this man that is inside of you, with whom you consistently swap souls and energy with. He is in lust with you, not love. He is a predator, and he has swooped down on his prey and demolished it. You allowed yourself to be used. You put your scent out there for a hungry dog to sniff you out and rip your meat to shreds, and, as soon as you understand the position you hold, the better off you will be. You cannot be mad at this man when it was you who gave him easy entry into the basement of your pussy, because you went shopping while you were hungry.

In conclusion, just know that being single does not mean that you have to be dumb or desperate. It's actually the best time for you to get to know yourself and sort things out in your head. Take time to get over that last heartbreak, work on your esteem if it's low, and spend time with your friends and family. Think about your future and what you want to do. Ponder on the mistakes you made and learn from them. Most of all, being single helps you practice self-discipline. When you practice and maintain self-discipline, men will respect you more, yearn for you more and want to be around you for reasons other than sex. And you will feel better as a woman, knowing that you are in control of whatever decisions you make. And it's not to say that you are a bad person. You're just being vulnerable, and some men often take advantage of that. Get control of your heart and hormones, so you can date without all of the vulnerability and bullshit. If you're going to have a hot, passionate sexual affair with someone, so be it, but learn to separate the game from the truth!

Gem
"If it's not worth fighting for...
why are you two always fighting?"

HOLD ON TO YOUR LOVE

When you meet someone, and you're consistently around this person, spending quality time, eventually you will catch feelings, right? You will then begin to do things so that this person will start to see what kind of long-term mate you will be. You are going to be supportive, loving, affectionate, and caring. Correct? You are going to maintain your person, keep yourself well-groomed and looking good. You will always, without a doubt, provide this person with a sense of security as far as where you stand, how you deal with things, and whatever you have to do to keep that person around. With some women, you want to show him that you are wife material, that you deserve to be treated a certain way, possibly proposed to, respected, and offered a long-term position. Getting fired is not on your radar.

But, in doing all of this to snag your man, you have to differentiate between the real you and the woman that is just doing these things to snag a man. It is very hard to maintain a caring, loving, domestic role when you are none of that. And it's okay if that is not you. But it is imperative that you showcase your strengths in the beginning of a courtship and, though it may not be the Susie-Homemaker that some men claim to love, and all that other domesticated stuff that men claim to need, he may very well possibly still want to love you and move forward with you because you are being real with yourself. Men love that! It may be your ability to solve problems, bring positivity into negative situations, your intelligence, etc. It doesn't have to be what you think the man wants. It's all about being yourself, learning the man while you're trying to earn him and incorporating your own strengths into the situation. It's all about give and take, learning and listening with compromise. The beginning of your relationship is the most crucial. You have to always continue to follow up with the behavior you exhibited from day one.

My belief is that, to be a good wife or a good mate period, you have to continuously grow and learn your mate. This goes for men as well. They sweep us off our feet. Then, they stop doing the things that they once did to keep us around, and we can't stand that, right? So you have to be the same way! You really must be in tune with your partner and stay there, meaning you have to really give a shit. The relationship can't be based on frontin' and lies and being catfish.

Also, the two of you have to really like one another, dig one another, get to know one another over and over again as the years go by. Things get stale, you go through ups and downs, but you have to remain friends and remain in tune with what is going on with your mate. You have to care! Also, understand that people change. Don't just assume that because you live together, "you know him like that." If you don't take the time to ask, talk and communicate, you will find that your mate is growing in areas that you know nothing about because you're too busy assuming. Don't think you know him or got him because you're his girl, his wifey, or his wife. It's not about titles! It's about earning your keep. All because you did twenty years in school does not mean you deserve that PhD. You could have been cheating your way through it, looking at other people's papers to get by, and winging it! You've been at your job for five years, but you're lazy, and you pass off all your work to your coworkers, but you wonder why you haven't gotten a raise yet. You feel you deserve one just because you were there for years. You feel cheated. Why? You didn't do anything to deserve a raise or promotion. You can't successfully be someone's mate without going through the different grades. Years mean nothing if you weren't paying attention to him/her all that time in class. But, when you are a woman that likes your man, cares about his needs, monitors his moods and grows with him, knows him more than he knows himself, your man will never forsake you, and he should do the same for you! You probably have moments where you are so frustrated with your mate because he just "doesn't get it." It is possible that he is taking for granted that he knows you, but you're changing! Right? Communication, my dear. Don't take your relationship for granted if you want it to last. By nature, men need nurturers. Yes, they need a woman that knows the difference between acting like his mother and loving him with a mother's love. People grow and change daily. You have to stay in tune with your mate. Don't think the man you met is the man you're waking up to this morning. You deserve to have someone that cares enough to follow your growth and wants to be a part of all that you do as well!

Don't believe that because of your surrounding circumstances everything is okay in your relationship. You don't want the only time he connects with you to be when he's inside of you sexually, right? Now, I know you and he live together, but it does not mean that you are connected. So what you have children? It doesn't mean that you are connected. Though you are married or live together, it does not mean that you are connected. Let me put it like this: If you have an iPod, sitting right next to a socket, not in the socket, but next to it, unplugged, and you leave it there for thirty days, the battery isn't going to charge just because it's next to the socket. No matter how close it is to that socket, it won't charge because it is not connected. So it doesn't matter how long you leave it there next to your bed, where you can see, and be sure that nobody else is touching it. That doesn't mean a damn thing if it isn't connected to you! You still can't use it, because it's not connected. It has no battery life! So what good is having that man in your house just because of kids, a ring, and all of these things when he is not connected to you? So take care of your love and let him take care of you, and, most importantly, stay connected!

Gem

"The Treasure Doesn't Do the Hunting"

SIMMA-DON-NAH

As women, we are designed from the gate to be everything that a woman is supposed to be in order to attract good energy, good men, good friends—feminine, loving, beautiful on the inside, adoring, and ladylike, strong, soft, confident, caring, trustworthy, sexy but tasteful, respectful and virtuous. Those characteristics that we were born with and (hopefully) raised with are enough. We come fully loaded and equipped. There is no need for anything more. Your confidence in you should be alluring enough to attract your mirror image. Often private revelations are better than public recognition. We don't need validation from a man or anybody do we? Simma don nah sweetie! Stop doing the most, when all you have to do is be still, love yourself, respect yourself then others will have no choice but to love and respect you as well. There is no sight more humbling than watching a woman get curved by a man, yet she is still just doing more than she ever needed to just to keep his attention.

First ladies, the key to getting everything you want from a man is to basically need nothing at all. There is no need to do too much too soon. Besides, every man isn't hubby material. Learn how to date, go out, have fun, explore your options, get chased for a while, send a few calls to voicemail, be nonchalant, and don't take your love life so seriously so soon! When you score, act like you've been in the end zone before. Just learn to have fun on the dating scene. You don't have to try to lock every man down that you think might be the one. If you take your time, you will find that you may not even want this man as bad as you thought you did. You may find out some things about him that are not worth fighting so hard to try to impress or keep him around. And don't try to take a man from his woman just because you see how good he is to her. Nine times out of ten, he won't treat you the same way. What's for her is for her and what's for you is for you. Just let things flow in your life! It's okay to just enjoy a man or three occasionally. Line 'em up blow 'em out like candles, girl! Date! Date! Date! And let the best man chooses you. Dating is healthy. It's like shopping. You get to walk around and choose things you like, return them if they don't fit, throw them in the closet and pull them out when you need them, or give them away to your friends if you have no use for them. Have fun until the one that separates himself from all the others reveals himself. But how would you know who is special enough if you don't give yourself the opportunity to choose?

Now, when you like a guy, it's okay to do a little bit extra to put yourself ahead of the other females that he may have in his stable. After all, it's about winning, right? But you have to practice some kind of self-control and maintain your emotions and self-respect no matter what. You have to take your time and give him a little at a time based on what he shows you. There are levels to this shit home girl, you know what I'm talking about? Below are four major components of a relationship that you should not do too much of before establishing where you stand with this man.

1. I do believe that if you're in a relationship, that your man should always, without a doubt, receive oral sex from you such as you should receive from him! Oral sex is something that is sacred. I know that sadly today's generation has totally taken away from how special giving and receiving oral sex really is, they say it's just a part of sex and everyone is doing it to everybody, but the reality of it is that it's not "just a part of sex." Oral sex is supposed to be reserved for that main guy, the one you love, the one that respects you and needs you, not the one you're trying to lure in. This guy who is not your man shouldn't be able to receive the benefits of your love making on such high intimate levels. You can't give him what you're yearning for you, understand? All because you want a man so bad, and you have an idea of how you want to make love to that special guy so bad, doesn't mean you should unleash that feeling or strong emotion on just any joe-shmoe. If you like this man and you want things to go further, why do you think he would want to lock himself down with you when he can get oral for nothing? As bad as you may want to feel his smooth and shiny penis against your lips, you have to ration the wretchedness. You can't give this man the "wifey" treatment by sucking on him every time you see him. This is how you spoil a man, and you don't need to be spoiling him like that when you don't even know where you stand. Find something better to do with your mouth until this man goes above and beyond to show you that you're his lady. #StaySuckaFree

2. Does he deserve Big Mama's secret recipe? The only time a woman cooks for man is if she is really trying to reel him in. The feeling of sitting that big full steaming plate of love down in front of your man and the smug look of satisfaction that appears on his face can't be matched. There is no sexual favor greater than that of feeding your man. But he is not your man. So why is he getting home cooked meals two to three times a week? Cooking is a deep act of intimacy in my book, (especially in African American homes). When you cook for a man, you are sending the message that you are trying to make this house a home for him. You're in that kitchen making these dishes with love because you want him to keep coming back. You want to feed him, make sure that he doesn't eat anywhere else. Keep his belly full because somebody told you that the way to a man's heart is through his stomach, right? But the beginning of this courtship is not the time where you should be in the kitchen. The two of you should be doing more talking about your cooking than actual cooking. Give him something to look forward to. He should be taking you out and courting you. Hell, he doesn't even belong in your foyer yet, let alone on your couch with a hot plate. Sylvia did not can her collards for you to be giving out her recipes to any lame that darkens your doorstep.

3. It's not about giving it up too fast when you're grown. If the chemistry is there and the respect is established and if it flows, then let it flow. Be free. You're no safer from the diss zone than the woman who makes a man wait three months. The issue now is how much sex you give a man in the beginning. You probably gave it up ten times in the first two weeks, sucking, cooking, and carrying on. But my Queen, if you saturate the "relationship" with nothing but sex in the beginning, then that's all the relationship is going to be about. The less you give, the more desired you will be. But again, some women have the fear of being left, so they overcompensate by having too much sex in the beginning. You have to ration that thang out, ladies. He's not your man; you guys haven't had the discussion about becoming a couple, so why invest so much of your time and body for him? What makes him so lucky?

4. You should never, ever, spend money on any man you're just dating. No, no, no! You are not proving that you're a real woman by footing the bill. No. Bad enough you have to spend money getting your hair done, getting a new outfit, paying the babysitter just to go out with this man. He better recognize and pay up. Stop taking these dudes out. What are you trying to prove? Be a lady, and let that man show you where his head is at. Definitely no dough for these men.

From a man's perspective, when a woman is doing the most too soon, he's probably thinking that you would do this for anyone or that you're desperate, which totally diminishes his thoughts of making you his girl. Keep in mind that you will never hear him complain. What man would? But peep game, Sis:

While you're smothering him with sex, food, and possibly the keys to your house, maybe to your car, and you're always available when he calls, and all the etc., there is a woman that gives him less, that he probably wants more of. Why? Peep Game: This woman keeps him guessing. She keeps him hungry. He's wondering where she is and how she's doing because she doesn't make herself so available. He wonders if she can cook because she's not offering up her Granny's special recipe on the first date. He's wondering what she likes to do, and he's going to try to figure it out. He's going to offer to take her places and try things with her to see if she might like it. He's going to chase her, court her, and try to be with her because men love to chase and to conquer. Tupac said it best, "I don't want it if it that's easy!" Men like women that they have to get to know in phases, a woman that keeps him guessing, that doesn't give up everything all at one time. To him, this woman is like the pancakes that you have to add eggs, milk, and a dash of cinnamon to. And you, my catering friend, are like the just add water version. You have made yourself so available that the thrill is gone. You're good, but he already knows what to expect from you, and he becomes content too early in the game! There is no doubt about it that he's going to begin to take advantage of you and treat you less than because, to him, you are coming off as thirsty, needy, clingy, doing the most for nothing because he knows he hasn't given you shit to even deserve all of this King treatment. So he's saying to himself, "Self, this bitch here will do anything for a man. I can get anything from her, for the low, low price of nothing!" And he's going to continue to do nothing and get everything he can from you. And this is how women wind up in situationships.

Showing him interest by simply giving him the time of day, conversing with him and having him around is enough to make him want to keep getting to know you. Give the guy a chance to show you what he thinks of you, how much he likes you, and what he has to offer you before you start planning weddings in your head and bringing him around family and friends. That kind of behavior can chase a man away! He'll start to feel pressured and smothered and forced into something that he probably isn't ready for at this very moment. It's okay to show a man love and make him feel good, but just remember that if you treat him like a celebrity, be prepared to get treated like a groupie!

Gem

"Give him your patience, not your pussy."

THE WAY TO A MAN'S HEART (HOW TO CUFF HIM FOR LIFE)

There are some women who spend a lifetime trying to figure out what they can do to keep the man they love in their lives forever. Some of you go to the extreme. You fake pregnancies; you attempt suicide; you throw tantrums, diagnose yourself with incurable diseases, dance around with headless chickens in the rain, put blood in his spaghetti, put his pubic hairs in a pot and sauté them in olive oil, and chant Missy Elliott's, Pussy, Don't Fail Me Now, three times while rubbing Noxzema on your face.

But I'm here to tell you that none of that will work if the man is:

1. Not into you

2. Not ready

Timing is everything when it comes to these men. If he isn't ready, there is nothing you can do to make him want you. Hell! If he doesn't want you, there is nothing you can do to change his mind, even if the time is right! You can save his mother from drowning, and all he's going to do is give you a high-five and be like, "Good looking on that saving my mom's shit," and that's that! Which is why it's not necessary to do the most. Simply, be you, and, hopefully, you are enough.

Now, they say the way to a man's heart is through his stomach....eh.... that plays a part. But it doesn't matter if you went to "Big Mama's School of Banging Pots and Licking Fingers," if that's all you have to offer, then that's all he will use you for. Bet you'll see his ass every Sunday for a good meal and that's about it. And then you got those females who use the power of the "P" to try and keep a man. Now I know we all like to think that our pussy is better than every other woman in the world. Nobody's box is wetter, tighter, cleaner, gushier than yours. I get it. But you're going to need more than a crotchless body stocking and a wet mouth whenever he comes over if you're trying to earn a spot in his life forever and not just for a night.

Let me let you in on a little secret that I learned about men through my studies:

Men love to have a woman that they can brag about and communicate with. They like to miss us. They like the mystery of having to wonder about us. They don't like it too much too fast. They like for a woman to be busy with her life and not so busy trying to be a wife. They like a woman they can chase, a woman with drive, a go-getter, a down-ass woman, a woman that's not just there when things are good but has the tenacity to be there through tough times as well. Sure, they love us sexy and attractive, but they desire a woman that is more than just breasts and ass. Sure you're a freak in bed. But you can't just give head all the time; you've got to use your head! You pretty much have to be an all-around, balanced woman to capture any man who is worth it. I mean, after all, this isn't too much to ask, is it ladies? Isn't a well-balanced man the kind of fella you want for yourself?

Which brings me to this: A lot of women want the perfect man, and your shit is half ass. You want Mr. Right to come to you correct, no flaws, no work needing to be done, money right, mind right, no bullshit, but what are you bringing to the table aside from your fat ass, which can be bought, so now every female is walking around with a fatty. So what else you got? Also, some women have no idea what being submissive means. Immediately, when you hear the word submissive, you think about a weak, stupid woman that listens to everything her man says. And that's why you don't have a man now or can't keep one because you're too independent and stuck on that dumb shit. The submissive woman is actually a strong, smart woman. She's strong enough to handle submission, and she's smart enough to know why she should be submissive and who to be submissive to. She knows exactly what to do to not only keep her man but keep him happy. Everything is about balance, ladies. You have to have a little bit of everything going on. Nobody says you have to be this Perfect Patty for him, but don't be so independent and hard core that you can't be soft for him. A hard chick makes a soft dick, remember that!

Enjoy making him happy. That's the way to his heart! Don't do it because you feel you have to do it. Do it because you enjoy it, and you think he deserves it. And, if you're with a man that doesn't deserve it, then why are you with him?

Whatever it is, just be genuine. A submissive woman knows how to cater to her man without losing herself amid it all. Even though this woman works a 9-5, has a million hustles on the side, children to take care of, a sick mother at home, and is going to college full time, she knows that her man has nothing to do with any of that. He is a separate job altogether, such as you should be to him! If he works, is running a business, is in school, doing all the things he has to do to be able to better his life, that is great, but he has to make the time to show his woman love. You have to make your man feel like a man, make him feel as if he is taking care of you, even though he can't take care of himself! A lot of you women are out there treating these lames like kings and can't even get their hair done from these fools. *File under don't be a dumb bitch* Then, by the time a good man rolls around, you're on your bullshit about not taking care of or catering to no man because you spent all your time trying to raise a grown man previously.

Aside from keeping the man, you first have to get him, right? There is but so much a woman can do to "make" a man want her. If a man sees you in his future, he will open his heart and let you in. Period. He has to want you on his own. He has to feel it in his heart that you are the kind of woman that will be there with him and for him through thick and thin. A man has to know that he can trust you, not on some shit about you fucking other men. That's minor in comparison to his real trust issues. He has to know he can trust you with confidential information, his emotions, his deepest thoughts, his plans, and his life. He has to look at you in a way that he looks at no other woman. He has to know that you will represent him to the fullest, whether he is around or not. Whatever it is that he desires in a mate, you must have those attributes. It doesn't make you unworthy that he doesn't want you, no matter how good of a woman you are, but you have to have the particulars for that particular man. He has to feel that you are loyal and faithful to his heart. And the shit with that is, if you're not a faithful, loyal type of woman, no man will ever see that in you, and you will get treated accordingly. But, for my down-ass, good hearted women, be cool, babies. It takes patience. Before you earn your man, you have to learn him. Men just act difficult because they like to put us through dumb-ass tests and what not. But men are babies on the low. They are needier than women and low-key more emotional and are very easy to please. Just get to know this man like the back of your hand by genuinely being interested in him, and it won't be hard. Fake chicks get fake results, remember that!

Figure out what makes him happy, what makes him smile, what makes him horny, what makes him mad, sad, annoyed, what turns him off, what turns him on, and act accordingly. Be a woman that is hard to replace! You have to get in this man's head without him even knowing. Play chess while these other women are playing checkers with their pussy and pulling out grandma's secret recipe, thinking this is the way to a man's heart. Because on some real shit, if you are the one he wants, he couldn't care less about you not knowing how to cook. He'll just be like, I love my baby with her non-cooking ass. And that's that.

In conclusion, cooking, cleaning, freaking, sucking...yeah, yeah, all that shit is what it is. These are things that make a man happy...temporarily, but it won't keep a man happy. When you want "him" to take you seriously and love and respect you, give him your patience, not your pussy. The real way to a man's heart is through your own. He has to feel how genuine you are. Show him how to love, and he will always love you and take care of you. Fellas, the same rules apply. If you want a woman to be loyal and faithful to you, then you have to make her feel and know that she is safe and protected at all times because women love protection and security.

Gem
"The blessing in being a woman is our ability to love over and over again even though we've been hurt over and over again. Don't let anyone block that blessing!"

ACKNOWLEDGE, ACCEPTANCE, AND UNDERSTANDING

The things that women endure in life can make or break us. This is very true. We, sometimes, live our lives according to our past and our upbringing, instead of living for today. Instead of learning from our mistakes, we yearn from our mistakes. Most women suffer from nostalgia. We want what we once had back. We want to go back in time and fix things and make it right. We want to be who we once were. We want a do over, and life isn't so. And then we hold on to our hurts. We, sometimes, find comfort in our pain, and we stay there, too afraid of going for the gold—our happiness—because we don't believe we deserve it, or we are too afraid to lose it once again, so we never bother going after it. We wear our pain as a badge of honor, ready to tell any man our story and how we got through it and what we will and won't do ever again in life. With that behavior, we harden as time goes on. We hide behind the things that hurt us, and we are afraid to be who we were born to be...women. But what you need to know is that, there ain't no nostalgia to this shit. When it's done, it's done, and we have to learn how to not be emotionless, but how to move on. There is a certain grace period that a woman should have to mourn over an emotional loss—be it a friend, a lover, or beyond.

Acknowledge the loss. Accept it. Understand it. Then, move on. In the next fifteen minutes, another one will be coming, and yes, it is that simple. We just make it harder because we refuse to accept things for what they are. What we need to learn overall is that most of the things that happen to us are not personal, so we shouldn't beat ourselves up. Sure, we are responsible for the things we do, people we let into our lives, etc. but we have no control over what people do to us! However, we do have control over how we react and how we allow it to affect our lives after it's all said and done. We have to learn to own our shit and stop giving "pain" so much power. The more we dwell on the hurt, the more it dwells inside of us and the harder it is to shake that shit. Some of us wallow in self-pity because we think that it's going to lure someone in to save us. Wrong. That's not the kind of attention you want from anyone that is supposed to genuinely care about you and want to be around you. You are nobody's sob-story. You are a success story! Move on from your past hurts and stand tall! Stop wondering what you did wrong and just acknowledge and accept that it is not working, whatever it may be! That bitterness you're feeling is being felt by every and anyone you encounter, and then you wonder why you can't receive love or happiness. Some of us are so mad and angry that we don't know how to speak like ladies anymore. We shut out anything good that is meant for us because we spit venom, we spit pain, and we spit resistance, all because of past hurts, fear, upbringings, and insecurities.

We've all been through hell, ladies, and, with that being said, shouldn't you have a blueprint by now on how to get out of hell should you find yourself there again? So stop feeling sorry for yourself. Stop waiting around for someone to save you from this pain. You are the only person responsible for you. Nobody owes you anything, and nobody is going to give you a map and guide you out of hell. You have to find your way around that place and remember the short cuts for the next time you unexpectedly wind up there.

What you also need to know is that you cannot hide from yourself. Your thoughts become your actions when you start believing it. Without even knowing it, we don't realize how we've pushed people away from us because of our negative energy. That energy spews out of us, whether we know it or not, and someone with the opposite energy will go the opposite way, be it a new female friend or a potential mate. The people that are bad for us will be attracted to us because that is the energy that we give off. Eventually, we find ourselves surrounded by so many people who are just as miserable as we are, and we don't think anything of it. We think it's the norm because there is no one around us to tell us that we are in a barrel of crabs. The next time you decide to sit around and dwell on past pains, ask yourself if the person that hurt you is sitting around dwelling on how much he or she has hurt you. They probably aren't.

A lot of our insecurities about men and friends stems from what we feel about ourselves inside and the things that we have done and allowed to happen to us. Once you have yourself in check, you will then be more than capable of building solid and honorable relationships with others. Don't ever tell yourself that you don't care about being in love or wanting that feeling again because you know and I know that it's a lie, and it's poisonous to think that way. If you keep telling yourself that, you will inevitably begin to live that way and you will get exactly what you asked for! Every woman wants to be loved, and, bigger than that, we want to love someone. We deserve to love someone. It's what we do. We love, we nurture, we nurse, we provide, we hug, we kiss, we make love, and we adore. Don't let anyone take the gift of giving away from you! In love, you have to take your chances and though it's a crapshoot, it is what it is! What doesn't kill us makes us stronger, right? And though it hurts, find out what went wrong, learn from it, laugh at your pain when you can. It helps to have people in your life that aren't judgmental and that you can be straight up with. Hiding what you go through will do you more harm than good. Talk it out, let it out, get answers, different perceptions from people who understand you. Don't be afraid to move on! Find the blessing in it all and always look at the glass as half full! No one deserves happiness more than you. So, slow down and smell the roses. Smile through your trials, dance in the rain, and laugh through your pain. And for the love of hip-hop, drop all that dead weight! Just drop it right now. Stop carrying all this around! Don't allow things you cannot control to make you bitter and angry. Our grace, our ways, our touch, our mind, our words are what makes us women, and, if we lose that, we have nothing. You don't want to surround yourself with individuals who have accepted defeat in one way or another, especially when you know deep down inside that you want to win again, or that you want to fulfill that dream, or that you want to rekindle that friendship or be in love again.

Our hearts are our joy, and, though we need to guard it and be mindful of who we give it to, it doesn't need to be guarded so much that nobody gets to experience the beauty of the love you have inside of you. You have to take risks in love. No matter how great you think your mate is, they are human, and they can hurt you, so your job is to protect yourself by also being human and understanding that shit does happen and that, when it does, you have to know how to move on. To give love is the greatest love, more so than receiving. It's about balance and knowing yourself, so you can understand the people who are around you and in your life. Some heartaches, we can't help; but some, we can certainly avoid. It's about being real with yourself! The blessing in being a woman is our ability to love repeatedly, even though we've been hurt repeatedly. Don't let anyone block that blessing! Once you acknowledge your pain, instead of trying to deny it. It will, then, force you to accept it. Once you accept the issue that you are faced with, then you can take the time to understand it. Once you understand it, you can move on with that knowledge and take the necessary precautions to avoid having to go through it again.

Gem

"You know that you have a good friend when you can tell her a secret without having to say,

"Don't tell nobody."

THE SECRET LIFE OF BITCHES...
SIX FRIENDS YOU SHOULD AVOID

From the time we were little girls, we experienced having a friend that was a hater, and, sadly enough, these baby haters turned into grown women haters, if they continue to hate themselves. Because that's all a hater is, a person that hates themselves, so they can't possibly love anything or anybody else...genuinely. But why hate on the next person because you choose to do dick with your time and she choose to get money, get better, get a life, and get ahead? Even worse is having someone you deem "close" to you that can't seem to be happy for you or anybody for that matter. How do you deal with that? It's so disheartening to have to deal with the energy of love vs. hate. What do you do? How do you cope? You love them. You've known them for a while. Hell! You might even be related to them! Whatever the case, sure they may have held you down during some trying times in your life, but the weather is always cloudy with a chance of shade and thunder stealing when it comes to this female, right? What do you do? How does that make you feel? Do you keep her around for the little bit of good she has? Do you not take it personal knowing that "that's just who she is?" or do you say "fuck this bitch. I'm over her bullshit!"

I mean nobody is perfect, and sometimes we are selfish, and we get in our own feelings and could care less about who we hurt and how we act. Sometimes, as women, we go through some real shit in life, and it's impossible to be happy at all, and we have to be selfish and fall back because we don't want to be around anyone doing better than us at the time. We need a moment to get our shit right before we resurface and join the Positive Party. I get it! None of us are angels, and none of us are exempt from doing stupid shady girl shit; however, there is a difference between being temporarily selfish and being a, dare I say it...hater. (I hate the term "hater" by the way, but you gotta call a spade a spade.)

We love our friends. We don't ever want to think that our girl, our bitch, our ace boon coon is jealous of us, doesn't want the best for us, or wants to see us fucked up. We will blame everybody but "her" when things look funny. "The devil trying to fuck up our friendship." No, sister-girl, you can't blame everything on the devil. Sometimes, it is what it is. Your home girl ain't shit, and you just don't want to see it because you love and trust her. Plus, she knows everything about you. These "friends" are no different from that man you love that you swear isn't cheating, would never do you dirty, will always have your back, and then boom, you get that call from the side-bitch that he's been dealing with since last June. Now, you're all "I can't believe it" and what not. It's the same thing! You are in a relationship with your friends as well, and, if you have a friend that fits any of the six descriptions below, you might want to rethink this friendship:

1. The "Enwords Ain't Shit" Friend

In the case of adult women, something is wrong when you hear grown-ass women still hollering, "Ni**as ain't shit." That is not healthy grown woman conversation, and clearly this woman has issues with men. Sure, ninjas ain't shit in some instances, but there are some good men out there, and, the fact of the matter is, we all want love, we all want a partner we can trust, and we all want happiness. But if you're being poisoned by a female who hates men, never has luck with men and doesn't believe she can be in a healthy relationship with one, you better believe she is going to low-key poison your relationships with subliminal hate, bullshit logic and negative energy in regards to this topic. So do yourself a favor and keep your love life to yourself when it comes to her. Avoid the unhappy and unlucky, she has nothing for you but war stories and a black heart.

1. The "Passive Aggressive" Friend

When it comes to friends, you have to understand that women should have different friends for different areas in their lives, as to not apply so much pressure to one friend to be "all things" to and for you. Also, understand that most "friends" only give advice based on what they are going through, not what you're going through, and, sadly, some women don't know how to be happy for others when they're going through hard times. This woman is the walking dead. Nothing ever works out in her life. She is always unhappy, complaining about something. Everything she says will have a negative or hateful vibe to it. She is very passive aggressive, and you will be very frustrated dealing with her after a while because you won't know if she loves or hates you.

She is the type that says, "I'm happy for you, girl. Just be careful though." "Congratulations, girl. I hope this works out for you unlike the last time." Things like that. This friend is doing what is called "projecting." She is projecting her negativity and anger, which stems from what's going on in her life, onto yours. This friend doesn't understand happiness and is probably comfortable in her own pain. Being happy is not a normal emotion for her. This "friend" has a condition called "Psychological Projection," which is a defense mechanism where a person subconsciously denies his or her own attributes, thoughts, and emotions, which are then ascribed to the outside world, usually to other people, like their happy go lucky girlfriends. In other words, she is a bubble bursting misery magnet, and you can't share your joy with her.... only your misfortunes. She just can't find the silver lining in anything! She is in her own damn way of being happy and she's going to make you feel like a fool for believing or make you feel guilty for being happy. She probably isn't even aware of what she is doing, so the grown-up thing to do would be to tell her what she's doing before you fall back from her, and, if she still does it after that, cancel this female because clearly, to this woman, water is not wet, and your feelings don't mean shit to her.

1. The 'I don't fuck with bitches,' Friend

She scares me. She really does because, as a woman, how do you not have a real bond or sisterhood with other women? "I don't fuck with bitches, because bitches be..." Let me tell you about a woman that is always ranting about how she doesn't fuck with other bitches. This is the most dangerous, insecure female in the world! First, Isolation is a sickness, and she is sick in the damn head and not only that, she doesn't want to see other females that are in a better position than her so that makes her a hater, and secondly, she is also afraid to see who she really is, in the females she attracts as friends so that makes her a weak bitch.

You need to get her the entire fuck out of your life! The next time you come across a female that's talking that bullshit, run! It's like taking a guy serious that's always talking about how bitches ain't shit. Would you date him? So why would you want to be friends with that kind of female when she is clearly talking to you! She is incapable of female interaction because she doesn't know how to interact with herself. She doesn't like herself. SHE'S A HATER, and all you're doing is enabling her and it's only a matter of time before you see for yourself how lousy this "friend" really is.

1. The "Emotionally Draining" Friend

THIS EMOTIONAL LEECH will sit on your couch and expect you to help her through every goddamn thing in her life. She can't think for herself. She needs your help in everything from what to wear out on a date to how to suck a dick. I mean, it's ridiculous. You do most of the talking in this friendship. You feel more like a therapist than you do a friend. You know what I'm talking about? And she gives nothing in return, so, after a while you get tired, you begin to resent her once you realize that this friendship is one-sided. She just sucks all the energy, knowledge, and information out of you, and, when she gets her life, she's gone, with not so much as a thank you card, and the bitch will only return when she's in turmoil again. You have to set boundaries with this "friend." She's a leech, and we all know leeches are suckers, and, when you feed a sucker, they just turn into a bigger leech. So stay sucker free!

1. The "Crab-Ass" Friend

This woman is codependent on your friendship, so any move you make that allows her to feel as if you won't have time for her anymore, she is going to shoot down in hopes of keeping you in that boat with the holes in it along with her. She doesn't really want to hear about that man that's making you happy because it's making her mad, so for every good thing you tell her about him, she's looking for a flaw in him to help her sleep at night. That new job opportunity you got? She's not happy about that either because it's going to take up your time. As much as she claims to hate to see you struggle, because sadly your pain is her pleasure. This female almost always has to "call you back," when you're in the middle of sharing some good news. No, you're not bugging. She just spilled hate on your garments. Your happiness just made her physically sick, so she had to take a leave of absence from the friendship until she feels strong enough to deal with all your greatness.

1. The "Down-Ass" Friend

You have to wonder why God even made these kinds of females. She is the epitome of what a frenemy is. They are around you 100% supporting you when you are down and out, while you're going through bullshit with these dudes, losing jobs, fighting with your siblings, going to court with your baby daddy, all that shit! They are right there, answering the phone whenever you call, coming over to "keep you company," lending that ear and that shoulder for you to cry on, giving so much of themselves to be there for you, and, of course, you will look at this woman as a great friend. You will tell everyone you know, "That's my bitch," because she was there for you! Nobody else was there but this ho. You feel as if you can tell this woman every and anything because she is there being a supportive, compassionate, loyal, loving friend. She prays for you, is there for you, wants the best for you. "Girl, I can't wait for you to find that true love, get that new job, get through this. You my bitch. You deserve to be happy. You deserve so much better. God is going to answer your prayers, girl. Watch!"

And by the grace of God and her prayers, what happens? You fall in love. You get a new job. Your baby daddy starts helping with the kids, and all of the issues you were hurt over are no more! And who better to share this news with than with that one down-ass bitch who was there, watching you struggle all this time? But every time you call to tell her all the good shit, this bitch is sleep. Sleep meaning, she doesn't want to hear about your happiness. But wait, she had tons of energy to watch you struggle and cry and offer her support, so what happened? This is where you learn that some people can only tolerate you when you're down, but when you're happy these muthafuckas ain't nowhere to be found! If you got a friend like this you should be very cautious. She is the same female that the minute the two of you stop speaking, she'll tell everybody how you ain't shit because she was there for you, and, now that you're happy, you think you're all that. Isn't that terrible?

So if a "friend" shows you this side of her after you guys stop speaking, consider yourself blessed that she is no longer in your life. The one thing that all of those women have in common is that they are some unhappy, insecure females, and we are too grown, too fly, too positive, and too blessed to deal with that mess. Amen? It is not your job as a friend to take the abuse. You are more than deserving of good friends. So make sure that she is not in your circle posing like a friend. Most importantly, make sure that SHE is not YOU!

Also, familiarity breeds contempt. It doesn't matter how great of a friend you think he or she is. Your safest bet is to keep things to yourself because that jealousy and envy shit is real. Once a fake female knows too much about you, she'll start calculating your moves, watching your pockets, checking out what your man is about, all for the sake of talking shit. These types of females are only around you until A) they get what they want from you, or B) YOU get what THEY want, you know what I'm talking about?

In conclusion, if you have good friends you can trust, be thankful and treasure them. It's a must that you surround yourself with like-minded individuals to avoid a lot of conflict. You are deserving of good friends, remember that.

Gem
"A friend of many is a friend to none."

WHY LONELY WON'T LEAVE YOU ALONE

Life happens regardless of your mood and what you're going through, honey. Despite what you may believe, time does not stop because you are having a bad day. You can bitch, moan, cry, and put it on the Goodyear Blimp. Just know that nobody cares about what you're going through as much as you do. And the more you complain, the more agony you bring upon yourself. I know you may feel as if the world owes you something for your blood, sweat, and tears, but it doesn't. And while you're on that bullshit, the relationships keep failing, and I'm not just talking about romantic ones. Your friendships fail; your work relationships don't exist; you career is at a standstill, and you keep telling yourself that it is everybody but you! And so quite naturally you give up on love and people in general.

For the life of you, you just can't find someone to love you. Your friends aren't coming around as much, and you are just miserable. Your energy, darling, is becoming toxic! You have to get to the root of the real issues here. Now, you're isolated from reality so much so that, when you do meet someone new, you get way more excited than you should because you're out of touch with reality, and then shortly after, the relationships fizzle out. You can list 100 reasons why this person didn't last, that friendship failed, you keep losing jobs. So many things they did wrong, so many issues they had that you just could not deal with. Every little thing they did annoyed you. The excuses as to why your love life is a revolving door is a long list of fuckery based on what other people keep doing wrong. The common thread is that it's never you. You're never the problem, right? But deep down, you know that it is you.

For whatever reason, you are scared. You spread yourself thin. You are all over the place, and the universe can't catch up with your feng-shui for shit! You treat yourself half-assed, so you attract half-assed people into your life.

Nine times out of ten, you're a people pleaser, and, instead of being you and being accepted, you choose to be what everyone wants you to be out of fear of being rejected. You probably have a million friends, but only two out of the twenty really care about you genuinely. You're doing too much to compensate for something... what is it? This behavior can cause you to be very (mentally/emotionally) drained, as keeping up any charade can be! No wonder you are so miserable. Baby! Let's get back to you! You may very well be a good person and have a good heart, but you have to stop running! Start peeling back the layers of negativity, low self-esteem, cynicism, heartache etc. that are allowing you to be doing so much of nothing to cover up your desire, need, and vulnerability, which are all essential to attract love and meaningful relationships! Putting a wall up to see who cares enough to break it down is childish. Nobody has time for all that.

So your first step toward being a better, more genuine, more fruitful you, is to own your truth! Stop making a Broadway production out of "other people's issues" to hide your own. Regardless of what you say about past lovers and others, the bottom line is none of them are around you because of you. Stop filling your body with empty calories, all kinds of junk, to temporarily fill you up, but within moments, you're empty again. All you have to do is stop for one second, be real with yourself and embrace the fact that you need to change, and, when you do, you will lose weight, meaning empty people, spot fillers, and vultures because we all know vultures only surround dying things. So don't be fooled or content with having many people around you, when, in fact, this is not a great thing but a dangerous thing, for you will never have time to see yourself if you're constantly hidden by everyone else.

You have yet to experience and to learn how to be content in solitary sometimes and not solidarity. Get with yourself, get with you, get to know you, learn yourself and stop blaming being lonely on having commitment issues. You do not have commitment issues. Stop lying to yourself. Own your shit! Be honest, the fact of the matter is no one is trying to commit to you because you aren't even committed to yourself. Take off the mask, look in the mirror, and see if you can stand the sight of your own reflection. Stop running from doorstep to doorstep for company. Relax, breathe easy, and bask in the ambience of your own great energy and learn to love being around you, not just or a day, but for a lifetime. Rejoice in yourself and then and only then will you be able to attract the greatness aka the mirror image of you. If you are uncomfortable in solitary, then you will be unsuccessful in attracting great relationships. Turn that quantity into quality, darling, and watch your energy and everything around you change for the betterment of you. Sometimes, you have to get rid of all the vultures flying around you and narrow it down to just a few important people and things. But it is always important to get into you. Increase honor with absence.

Gem
"When I was a child, I spoke as a child. I understood as a child. I thought as a child, but, when I became a (wo)man, I put away childish things."

PIGEON POLITICS

This grown woman who refuses to grow up has the same mentality in her thirties that she did as a teen. You know who she is. She's judgmental, gossipy, messy, and always into some kind of teenage shenanigans. She claims to want a good decent man, a better way of life, better friends but can't seem to achieve these goals because she just won't grow up. Her mind has not expanded beyond fast cars, white T's, hardcore rap music, and her bitches. She stays in weed clouds, and you can find her at the nearest rap concert surrounded by "some real ni**as."

This woman probably leaves her kids at home, so she can go lay up under some dude or is constantly moving men into her home. Nine times out of ten these men aren't doing anything for her but selling her dreams and ragging her pussy out. Then, he sends her home to her children with not even a dime to put food in their mouths or pay the babysitter. This chick probably doesn't work, is still trying to beat the system, and is content with the $161 a month they give her every two weeks alongside some food stamps. This female would spend her last $50 on a bottle of Patrón to bring to her home girl's house instead of using that money to put groceries in her fridge. She has a diet of Crown Fried Chicken and cigarillos. This female has probably never left her hometown, afraid to explore a world outside of police sirens and dirty snow. This woman so desperately wants to get out of the hood to see and do things, but to her, it's meaningless. What's the point? She's still reppin' her block and her borough, running around with her day one bitches, fighting other cliques of day one bitches. Niggas will never be shit to her, being a side bitch makes her world go round, sleeping all day and fucking all night is what's up to her, going to work is not her thing, winging it and doing whatever to get money is a way of life for her. Any basketball wife or reality TV "star" is her idol and BET is her kid's babysitter.

Unfortunately, a lot of females from the hood are globally physically and mentally challenged and they behave this way because they know no other way. They haven't left the blocks or benches in years, if ever! You claim to not have the finances, oh but yes you do. But you'd rather spend it on what means the world to you vs going out to see the world. When you get your refund check, the first thing you do is invest in Brazilian hair and a new bag, to walk around the hood and post it on Instagram calling yourself the "baddest bitch." I mean, what gives? If you think about all the money you spend on bacon, egg, and cheese sandwiches, vanilla Dutches, Brazilian weaves, and Pro-Style gel in a month, that's a plane ticket to somewhere nice. And I'm not talking about New Orleans for All-Star weekend either. There are a million different worlds right where you live, why not begin to explore the world right outside of your door? You've been seeing the same shit day in and day out. You're still fighting and wishing a bitch would. When will you stop being a bubble goose god and get a grown woman coat and go to a play, go to a ball, go to a vineyard, and go do something different! Because on top of everything else, you complain about the men in your life. I mean, there are some good men that come from the ghetto. Let me not even try to front. Being hood doesn't mean you aren't any good. The ghetto is a beautiful place so full of promise. So much inspiration grows from the streets, but you have to learn how to take what you don't have, mix it with what you need, and create a better life for yourself. You have nothing but prayer and imagination when growing up in the hood. Take that and make it a reality. Nothing is impossible. You can't use the ghetto as an excuse to fail when so many of us have come from nothing.

Who's your inspiration? Who do you idolize? Is your mom, nana, an older sis, an auntie around? What about a neighbor that you watch come and go every day or an old teacher. Perhaps, your ex-man's mother? Is there anybody around you doing anything that gives you a little bit of hope to want more out of life? If not, then let's take the examples of women who you probably look up to that come from where you come from and look at what they did with it. Okay, you have, Keyshia Cole, who is an alleged crack baby and foster child; Mary J. Blige, who grew up fatherless and abused drugs and alcohol and was a victim of domestic violence; Fantasia, who was a single teenage mother that couldn't read; Lil Kim, who was deep throating for C-notes and fucking for car keys; Nicki Minaj, who rapped her way from pissy staircases to stardom; hell, even Michelle Obama came from the dirty south side of Chicago to become a successful attorney and is now the First Lady of the United States of America. All of these women came from the bottom and knew they deserved a better life, and they went for theirs. Now these women, though not unflawed, cleaned up the areas in their lives where they wanted to see the most improvement in, without compromising who they are! So what you have to do is get serious about your life, believe in yourself a little more, and put away childish things.

You're wondering where the real men are. They are all probably somewhere hiding from you! Who wants to deal with an immature woman who doesn't want to grow up? What decent man is going to be attracted to you when you're still in the clubs drinking, acting all crazy, can't hold your liquor, cursing people out, hanging in the VIP section being a lounge lizard? Ho-sting parties and what not? You can't attract a decent man if you're not living decent. That's just how it goes, hon. This woman that keeps complaining about "where the real niggas at," does not care enough about herself to not want to get caught up in the cycle of instability that a knucklehead provides. This is probably the only kind of man she will attract because she's a knucklehead her damn self. And I know you want more, who doesn't? But you have got to break away from that way of thinking that has you stagnant. Surround yourself with people who are about that life that you want to live. Stop settling for a piece when you can have it all. Learn how to eat better!

You can't be a grown-ass woman still striving to be a True Thug's Wife. It's over. You are grown. Leave the bullshit alone that obviously hasn't gotten you anywhere. Know your worth! Don't be the "Old Bitch" in the club, dressed like a twenty-year-old, still trying to pick up rappers, rocking the mink coat you bought with your income tax during a summer sale twenty-five years ago. Don't be that ole silly broad that'll risk your job, for the sake of a man by doing something illegal. Don't be that female going to your friend's man's house to help her fight his side bitch. Don't be that girl any more... It's time to be a woman and put away all childish things.

Get a pen, write down the things that you want for yourself, and then write down the obstacles that you believe are in your way, then write down what steps you can take to knock down those roadblocks. Spend the next few months working on these things and don't stop until you see progress. When the people around you begin to fall back from you, you know that you're on the right path. You are going to feel uncomfortable. It's going to be touch and go with loved ones, and they won't understand your change, your growth, or your new outlook on life. They are going to say you're acting funny. They are going to say that you changed. They are going to say and do things to make you feel guilty for wanting more. Don't fall for that shit! Don't you stop growing! Encourage your best girl to come along with you for the ride. And, if she doesn't want to grow with you, unfortunately, you have to learn to leave people behind, but you have to grow, honey, and don't let anyone stop you. As a matter of fact, to hell with anybody who's trying to stop you. You deserve greatness and all that this life has to offer. Just because you're from the ghetto doesn't mean you can't grow and find love and be respected! It is time to put the pedal to the metal. Mow down and roll over anybody who is trying to get in the way of that. The choice is yours. I hope you choose you!

Gem
"A good girl blushes when she watches porn.
A bad girl smirks because she knows she can do it better than the girls in the video."

SEX AND THE CAREER WOMAN

Mmm hmmm, remember when you first met him, and you knew the night had come that you were going to give into him? You shaved, did your Kegels, bought a sexy outfit to wear under your clothes, and you put the plan in motion to give it to him better than any other woman he had ever encountered because you wanted that man to keep coming back. You liked him, you were turned on by him, and it reached the point of the two of you having sex. You turned up Missy Elliott's "Pussycat" song and sang as you got dressed, and it worked! You put that good, good down on him, and he never let you go after that. Yes, honey, once you bone him, you own him! He became your man, and the two of you have been doing just fine. But somewhere along the way, things changed. Now, I hear you, mama. You are a career woman. You work hard. You're not just home laying on your back all day playing on social media. You're a wife, a mother, a girlfriend, a student, and, without a doubt, you have to make time for your kids and yourself. Your man sees you working hard, he loves that his woman isn't a slouch, and so, with that said, almost every day, he's excited and turned on, hoping that today his baby won't be so tired or occupied with life that she neglects her duties as a wife. And almost every day, your man is disappointed, not turned off, because he knows you're working hard, but he's disappointed that yet again, he can't get no head, no nookie, no nothing. Your man will empathize with you all of five minutes about your long day and you're to do list but understand that there will come a time that after three minutes of hearing about your business, anything after that will sound like an excuse or a complaint to him. And sure, your man loves you to death, but he has needs. What do you expect a man to do...honestly? You don't want that do you? You love your baby. You want to make him happy, so what do you think you should do?

Sacrifice! You have to get out of that funk and turn your man back on...and turn yourself back on as well! The work clothes, the food stains from the baby on your shirt, the frumpy house pants and same ole tired hairdo has got to go. You don't feel too sexy do you? Understand that men are visual creatures, so you have to keep him looking at you. I'm not saying you have to wake up at five in the morning and beat your face but don't be so lazy! I'm sure he loves you just the way you are, but change up that hairdo, get a mani and pedi with a burst of new color on your nails, buy some new perfume, a new piece of lingerie, get those eyebrows snatched, pull your hair back, and give your man face, honey! Wash off all that work, mommy, and student funk, and be a single, sexy woman for the night, for your man. Sacrifice one night of sleep, one night of studying, and show him the woman that used to do it all to impress him in the beginning, I know that he's looking for her and misses her! You're going to be a little hurt when you see him looking at other women because his lady isn't giving him anything to look at home. All men look at other women, so what? They watch porn. They talk shit when they are out with their friends. They reminisce on old flames all the time. They look at other women when you guys are at the mall together. It's no big deal. But the only reason why you'll be mad is if you know you don't have yourself together. Even when he does look at other women, it's not with yearning eyes wishing his woman looked like her. He's looking like most men do, and then he's reminded of what a bad chick he has at home. And he's going to come home to you, but not if you're dressed in a Free the L.O.X t-shirt, funky leggings with blunt breath, and Hennessey fumes coming out your pussy. Make time and take a break from that busy schedule and breathe. Switch up the routine and do something new. Do something spontaneous. Show up to his job if you can and give him some lunchtime loving if you know you might be too distracted at home. Reupholster your pussy and get a Brazilian wax or a cute tattoo down there, put his name on it, take him to the strip club, and buy him a few lap dances. Do something!

Sex is very important in a relationship to men and women, make no mistake about it, but these men aren't going for the excuses! It is your job to stimulate your partner sexually as much as possible to keep them satisfied and occupied in that department. As long as the two of you still like one another that shouldn't be too hard. Now I say "like" because you can love someone to death, but you don't have to like them. You may not be able to give it to him all the time. This is understandable as a busy career woman, but, when you do make the time to have sex with your man, give him some quality time. Don't rush it. Allow him to enjoy you and enjoy him as well—you deserve it! Just always remember what you did to get him.

He fell in love with that girl, and he admires the hard-working woman that you are. That is why he is with you. But tonight you need to fuck your man like you're trying to get the mortgage paid. Tired or not, busy or not, make the time to take care of your man's sexual needs, or someone else will. Good Luck!

Gem

"Grown women don't want drama. They value their time way too much and would rather spend it doing something beneficial to their happiness."

THIS IS FOR THE COOL IN YOU

Every man loves the cool girl, doesn't he? You're like one of the fellas. You kick it, throwback shots, sit around while they play PS4s and might even join a weed cypher with him and his boys. You know all the lyrics to the latest rap songs, and you got a connect for damn near everything he's trying to get into. The fact that you're so cool and resourceful makes you feel so wanted and need and good right? He's always calling on you, leaning on you, hollering at you for something? You feel needed but your desire to be accepted by a man has you blind to the fact that you're being used. First of all, no man wants a woman that kicks it like one of the fellas. How serious do you expect a man to take you if you're calling him "son?" Or if you're sitting around with him and the fellas talking about the hottest rapper that's out, or if your running to the store to get cigarillos for him and his mans, or if you are always voluntarily leaving his house directly after having sex because you don't want to smother him. You want to be so cool. Let me explain to you how this shit will backfire on you each and every time.

Men generally want a woman that doesn't nag, doesn't give any problems, doesn't beef about things, and lets him be a man, whatever that may entail. So when a man comes across a woman with all these attributes, he feels as if he's hit the jackpot, but at what cost to you? The cool woman is so cool though, that she accepts way more than she should from any man. She wants to be loved for what she believes a man wants, so she sacrifices her own wants and needs. She doesn't speak about the fact that their relationship status is casual when she wants more. Yet she deals with the fact that he sees other women, that after a year he still isn't ready for something serious. She's so cool that they can kick it without commitment. She is so cool and down with the fellas that it's okay, and it's not.

My belief is that this woman is afraid of getting hurt, so she hides behind this "cool chick" persona and deals with all the indiscretions with a smile and a "I'm good!" She's straddling the fence and figuring, "Well, if I know this and that about him already, then I know what to expect, so if and when it happens, I won't be mad or hurt because I already knew what it is." Oh, but when that jones comes down, you're not so cool, are you? Imaging giving so much of yourself to someone and feeling paralyzed when it comes time to ask them for more. Imagine working on a job for three years, never being late, doing an outstanding job, making your boss so happy but feeling as if you don't want to rock the boat by asking for a raise. Now, don't get me wrong. She may very well be a cool chick, but, as a woman, when you want more from a man, you are supposed to speak up and voice your feelings because a man is not going to say anything. He is going to keep that "cool" relationship right where it is and continue to benefit from you, without having to give you anything in return. Now, you're going to wind up getting your feelings hurt because you played it cool instead of expressing how you really felt out of fear of "turning the man off" and risking him not liking you anymore. What happens after that is, we spend a lot of time trying to convince ourselves that this "relationship" is right.

We deal with the bullshit issues that this man has because we are so cool. We are the cool, understanding chick. We sit down and kick it with him about why he does what he does, even if what he is doing is hurting us. Why? Because we are so cool and down, and "we know how men think." We know how the boys get down. We understand and try to convince ourselves that we are one of them. Reality check, sweetie. We are NOT one of the boys when it comes to matters of the heart. Quit being so understanding of this man's predicament, whatever it is! Stop telling yourself, "I ain't even mad at him." You should be mad at him for stringing you along! This man is treating you like a yo-yo. On one hand, he is feeling you, right? I mean he can sit back with you, have drinks, laugh, talk about anything, be himself, and do whatever, and what man doesn't love that about a woman? Not to mention, this man can (probably) fuck you whenever he wants. It doesn't matter that you haven't seen him in days or that he has a girl that "it's not like that" with, or the fact that he told you he isn't ready to settle down, but, when he's ready, you will be the one, but, in the meantime, let's just enjoy each other, which simply means, you'll never be my girl for whatever reason he has in his head, but I enjoy fucking you with no strings attached. He gets all these privileges without having to give you anything in return, so why wouldn't he keep you around? But like a yo-yo, he pulls you close to him for his own benefit, then drops you and leaves you hanging when things begin to get too serious.

So now you're all frustrated because you put your "cool" before your "couth," and he isn't trying to hear anything outside of that. Once you begin to express your disdain for the things he's doing, you're looked at as a nag, a bug. "C'mon man, don't do this. I thought you were cool. That's why I fucked with you because you don't beef about the shit that other women do." That is not a compliment. That is a slap in the face! What's cool is a woman that speaks her mind and knows how to walk away if the man is not willing to give her what she deserves. That is what real men find cool! Only a sucker will keep a woman around, manipulate her into thinking that his half-ass attempt at a relationship is all she deserves and needs. And if he likes you or cares about you, he will respect the fact that you're not settling, and he will either come correct or keep it moving. Either way, you win! There is a very thin line between playing cool and playing fool. Next thing you know, he thinks you're so cool, so he continues to do the things that tear you apart—the neglect, other women—while you're sitting there, shelving your feelings. He will continue to have a million relationships "around" you but not with you, and why? Because he thinks that you're so cool and that you will understand.

In being the cool girl, you will accumulate a lot of male homie-lover-friends, unfulfilling situationships, and pain. These relationships will have a spark when they start but trying to maintain your cool after catching feelings is a hard persona to maintain. Nobody deserves to feel unappreciated after putting in so much time and effort with a man and being so cool. Heartbreak doesn't seem like such a fair exchange for a woman who has offered up so much to make a man comfortable and happy. Now you're alone, frustrated, and full of resentment toward a man who (that yes he should not have taken advantage of your coolness, your heart, and what you felt was the right approach to keep him happy) pretty much did use you to his advantage. He had his cake and ate it, too, on your dime, and the minute shit got real, and you revealed how you felt, he ran because now you're no longer an easy, "cool" task for him. You now come with "responsibility," a responsibility that YOU should have made him aware of off the rip, instead of being "the cool girl." It's okay being cool with your man or the guy you're dating. But what is NOT cool is hiding how you feel, dumbin' down your true you and ignoring your own heartache and unhappiness to make any man happy or anyone happy for that matter. The cool in you is a gift, a prize, and a special part of you that the man who deserves it should only get to see. You don't have to act like one of the fellas to be cool! When dating and looking for a serious relationship, don't EVER be too cool to say how you feel and express your wants and needs out of fear of "losing" him. This is exactly how you will be able to separate the boys from the men. It's not cool being the cool chick when you want and deserve more!

Gem

"No need to demand with words what you can simply command with self-respect."

HORITHIANS 3:14

Let me just say this. Most, not all, but most women and even men go through a ho phase in life. They are trying to find their way, their niche. They are trying to satisfy a feeling inside of them that can only be cured with promiscuity. It is a natural progression into adulthood and maturity to date, have sex, explore and do some wild crazy shit. On the other hand, some people just love sex and having a variety of different partners. But being a ho is based on not who you do, but how you do it, am I correct?

Let's use Kim Kardashian as an example. She was introduced to us via a sex tape. Now, that was a very tacky situation, but Ray J was her man at the time, right? How many of you females made a sex tape with your man or a guy you were in a "Situationship" with? Now, sure she "leaked" her tape for financial gain, but does that make her a ho? We have seen all the men she's dated, so because we can count the number of men that we know she's been with, does that give the public the right to call her a ho just because we know her body count? Can you be considered a ho if you've slept with ten men but all of them claimed you in some kind of way? Well, if Kim was a ho, she successfully deleted her ho-ness by becoming a mother and settling down. Ctrl+Alt=ho-nessBeGone!

Now, let's get into this deletion of your ho-ness shall we? Deleting your ho-ness is like being a former crack head. You can't delete all that crack you smoked in '85! However, you can get clean, apply for jobs, and become an honorable member of society, right? You can move to a new state, become a new person, and nobody in that town would know that you used to be a crackhead unless you unfortunately smoked up all your teeth and Obamacare didn't kick in yet. But, if someone knows you well enough to remember you being a crackhead, they will forever hide their valuables around you off impulse. Such as a woman will hide her man around you if she knows you used to be a ho. She's not chancing you relapsing on her dick or dime. It's unfair, but you will always be "ho ass Keisha from Building 120, Apt 3C." That's messed up because you've paid your debt to society. Like a juvenile criminal, you did your time, right? You weren't in your right frame of mind, you were out there committing all kinds of crimes, but you grew up! You learned the errors of your ways. You stopped the bullshit, and you shouldn't be held accountable for things you've done in the past if you already paid your debt to society, correct? So what do you do? You switch up the places you hang out and the people you hang out with. You disassociate yourself from the people you used to know that's on that same ole bullshit, and, in due time, you will be recognized as a do gooder, and, with all that being said and done, you can request that your record be expunged! Well, it's the same process that you have to go through to delete your ho-ness.

People do change, and you have to give them credit for that. Promiscuous women run out of gas eventually. When those walls start to collapse like the Twin Towers, you know it's time to have a seat. (Hopefully, get some Vaginoplasty/Pussy Rejuvenation, if you can afford it). But you will always have a pusher man out there, trying to remind you of what a ho you were by constantly throwing it up in your face. He will constantly throw up how you hung in La Marina all summer and let some cats touch it in Miami. He will cause you to relapse and give up all hopes of not being a ho anymore. So stay clear of anyone who doesn't believe in or support your attempt to change, grow up, and slow down your dick-in-take etc. I mean, no woman wants to walk around with a vagina that looks like a scream mask. In order to delete your ho-ness and regain your dignity, here are three imperative steps you must take in order to begin the process.

1. You gotta stop hanging with other hos. Dawn, Mo-Mo, Tish—all those bitches gotta go. No more poppin' bottles in VIP with these hos, running to All-Star Weekend, hanging out in La Marina.
2. You have to put the pussy on pause. No frivolous fucking for, at least 90 days. Put that pussy in rehab. Go under the radar and get lost. Increase your honor with absence!
3. Delete all the dudes that smutted you out from your phone. Block the numbers, all that. There should be no contact with men period.

You must, without a doubt, wipe away your own traces of ho-ness first and foremost. Reinvent yourself, spend some time alone, and get to know you, replace the urge to suck a dick with eating a ten-cent bag of sunflower seeds since you like salt so much. But if you're ho level is in code orange, then you should move to another town and start over fresh. If nobody knows you, then nobody can judge you, so start over and be great! Get that record expunged, girl! You can do it! Because there is nothing worse than a young ho that turns into an old ho. Let your vagina breathe and get used to just one mic. Let it hug just one muthafucka. Stop giving out group hugs with your pussy.

In conclusion, be who you want to be, sleep with how many men you want, own your shit, be great with who you are, but slow down because at the end of the day you are a woman. You're not like the fellas, and we are not equal to them in that aspect no matter how much we want to believe it. We cannot do what the boys do. We can't give our bodies away and switch up partners like it's nothing. That's just how it is, and you shouldn't want to be like the boys. Your body is precious. Protect it. It's never too late. You deserve a second chance at being great and don't let anyone hinder your transformation. Go on and be great, baby girl. You deserve it!

Gem

"Respect Yourself... Don't Reject Yourself."

WHAT MAKES YOU SO SPECIAL?

So many single ladies out there want a better life, want to be a wife but don't know how to be a woman. Day in and day out women lie to themselves and act as if relationships are not important, because in this society, we have become brainwashed to think that being in a meaningful relationship is a waste of time because everybody cheats. Deep down inside, you want to be loved, you want to give love, but you put up this front as if you don't want to be bothered. "Ain't nobody got time for that," right? Outside influences, even past loves, play a role in your present. Why? Because you feel as if your pain is a badge of honor! Every chance you get you can talk about what you've been through, what you've dealt with, how you handled it in an attempt to let future lovers know that they can't phase you. You sound crazy. All you're doing is giving them ammo to hurt you and why not? A bad bitch, strong woman like you can handle that shit right? Isn't that the message that you're sending out to these men? Holding on to the past hurts and allowing it to affect your present life will only make you bitter, darling! Then what happens after that is we build up this sense of entitlement because you are a woman, and you've been through too much and you ain't taking any bullshit. You instantly deserve a good man for all of the things you have gone through in the past that has nothing to do with the new man that you're trying to will into your life, and, for that reason alone, you feel as if you don't have to put in the work to get or keep a good man because of all the shit you've been through. Am I correct so far?

Some of us women got too much shit with us, and guess what sweetie, good men are not trying to deal with it, period. Just like you feel a sense of entitlement, so do these "good men," and that's only fair. Be honest. Your attitudes and could use some adjusting. Your morals could use a quick dunk in the waters of Lake Minnetonka, your style of dress could certainly be upgraded from nasty to classy, your priorities, and most of all your ways of life could use some coaching. There is always room for improvement no matter who you think you are. Oh, wait! Let me guess, not you, because you're perfect. So there is not one thing wrong with you that can turn a man off?

You know...women are funny. When we want and love a man so much we will go to great lengths to try to change him so he can be a better man. Why don't we love ourselves just as much to change our ways so that we can be a better woman? Be honest with yourself. Look at yourself in the mirror and say, "I am not perfect! I have flaws! I may not see them, but someone else might." It's okay to not be perfect! Just learn to dig a little deeper into that shallow soul of yours and find the problem, slap it down on the table, and look it in the eye. Own your shit! The next step is to figure out what defines a good man before we step out to begin our search for one. Then, we have to be real about our expectations and our current situations, and not ask ourselves "Am I good enough?" but "What can I bring to the table?" Yes! Aside from breasts and thighs, what can you bring to the table? You are not special because you are a woman. What do you have to offer? What would a good man want from you, and do you have those attributes? In our community, too many of us put money before morals, money before respect—money before everything. Meaning, if the man has that paper to provide for us, we don't care how he treats his kids, how he treated his ex, his momma, where he's been, where he's going, what he's up to, or who he's with. We think a good man is a man who's got money to take care of us, so you need to be clear on what a good man is to YOU and can you match his goodness to avoid conflict down the line.

As cliché as it may sound, a good man is a man that first of all is so lost in Christ, that he has to seek Him in order to find you. He doesn't have to be a Holy Roller, but, ladies, how many of you honestly are too afraid to ask a man if he believes in God, what his religious beliefs are, and if he would go to church with you? How many of us hesitated in doing so because we didn't want to turn the man off? Well, then, there is your answer.

1.) You aren't complete enough as a woman, if you're afraid to bring God into the equation to even seek a good man.

2.) He damn sure isn't good enough if you feel as if he is giving you the vibe that you can't ask him about spirituality.

Your relationship is doomed from the start if the two of you are unwilling to bring God into the relationship from day one, be it a friendship or something more. Everything starts with God. I don't care how thugged out ole boy is or how much of a ho you are. Everything begins and ends with God. Who else can you run to when you need to be stopped from going upside that man's head for doing something dumb? Who else do you run to when you don't want that man to leave? Who else do you run to when you want to thank someone for placing such a great man in your life? So ask that man what his religious beliefs are. Set that tone that you are the woman God speaks of in Proverbs 31. Let it be known (minus the neck rolling, gum chewing, and 'tudes) the kind of woman you are through your actions. If he chooses to overstep those boundaries and make you feel as if he is not willing to give you the respect you deserve, then move on. He showed you who he was—believe him. Too many of us stick around from early on to prove a point or to show a man what we're about and how he needs to treat us. No, sweetie, that is not your job to do so. Disrespect is not part of the equation. Sometimes, a man doesn't know, so he tries his hand. But what is on the agenda of a man who would even try to get away with disrespecting you? Whatever it is that you want out of your mate, you have to be capable of giving. You are what you attract, so, if you keep attracting bullshit dudes, then perhaps it's time to reevaluate yourself. Just know that simply being a woman doesn't make you any more special than anybody else. It's like having a Benz without any tires. It looks good but what can it do, what is it worth and where can it take me?

Gem

"Sometimes there is no right answer.

You gotta just do what you feel is right and deal with the townspeople later."

WHEN PILLOW TALK GOES WRONG

Isn't it nice when you can lay up in bed with your guy and share stories about your life, the limited edition about your past, what you and the girls did last week, and what happened at work on Monday? There is no better joy than being best friends with your man, right, ladies? I understand that when you and your mate are really close, you share lots of details with him because you trust him, and you expect your mate to not use it against you. But the fact of the matter is, it's not that way. You cannot pillow talk and share everything with your mate, especially information about your friends.

Some men and some women suffer from extreme bitch-assness, and though there is no cure for this disease that has spread maliciously throughout our hoods, doctors are working diligently on a cure for this horrible disease that has destroyed friendships, partnerships, businesses, and the like. Men who feel very comfortable with their lady, laying up with her and sharing intimate details about their friends, are the corniest men on earth. You don't do that. But (most) men have no common sense after they bust a nut. It's like taking candy from a baby. In some cases though, the man can simply feel that his lady is a cool chick and that she won't hold anything against his homies after he tells her some personal stuff. I mean, it's okay you just have to know your partner enough to know that they can handle this kind of information without judging. UNFORTUNATELY, though... in the case of women, those who pillow talk about their girls often always have another agenda. They feel some kind of way about the female that they are kicking dirt on to their man. These types of women are weak, and a weak bitch is a lousy bitch, and a lousy bitch will try to make other women seem lousier, so she won't seem as lousy.

Women who pillow talk about their close friends normally do this, so they can seem like the prize out the bunch, or she doesn't want her man to look at her friends in an attractive light because she is insecure. Another theory is that the pillow-talker is envious of her friends living the "single life" while she is in a (miserable) relationship. What other reason do you have to lay up and have pillow talk with your man, and tell him so much sensitive shit about your friends? What are you getting out of dry snitching on Tanisha because she sucks dick on the first date or Shelly because she cheats on her man when he's outta town? It doesn't matter how "cool" you are with your man, some things are better left unsaid. Your man does NOT tell you everything. Please believe me. I don't care if he swore to his dead homie, his sick grandmother, or said word to B.I.G. He's lying if he tells you that he tells you everything! Do you think he tells you about half of the things his boys do when they are out? No, and you know why? Because he knows that you will judge him by what his friends do, and that's exactly what your man is going to do to you when you tell him all of the trifling things that your friends do! Now you're stuck at home arguing with him every time you go out with Tanisha or Shelly because he thinks that you're going to be out there sucking dick and cheating. And that's not fair now, is it? But you asked for it when you opened your mouth.

Side Note: Your man doesn't want to hear half the shit you tell him about your friends, but he will select certain things that you tell him to use against you later. The only reason why he wants to hear about your girls is so that he can know what kinds of bitches they are, so he can hook them up with his mans or potentially develop a down low situation with the bitch himself. And if your man is a low-key creep, you will soon find out! So keep your mouth shut and stop being insecure. Keep your friends and the life you had before your man separate, and definitely don't tell him how your friends are hos because he will go and find out for himself how much of a ho she really is, and you'll only have yourself to blame for that!

PS Be a better friend.

Gem

"It ain't where he's at, it's where he wants to be."

THE FIRST WIVES CLUB

As women, and more so as mothers, we have to be strong for our children, mentally and emotionally when the relationship between us and their father has come to an end. We have to hold the fort down and make sure we protect our children by any means necessary even if it means, worst case scenario, cutting daddy out of the picture. When these relationships fizzle and we are left holding a baby on our hips, it is up to us to wipe our noses, poke our chests out, get those better paying jobs, make that house a home, put that smile on our faces for our children and be the best mothers we can be with or without daddy being present. We must soldier on. That should be our main priority. But the ladies of the First Wives Club (hereinafter known as FWC), are on some Jennifer Hudson and "I am telling you"Shit. They're not going anywhere! They believe that it's going to work out because they had his first kid, his first son, been with him since they were sixteen, all this dumb shit. The ladies of the FWC continue to let their baby daddies hit it, hindering themselves from finding true happiness, all because they were there first and they refuse to let this man go. The women of the FWC need to take a page out of the book of Misa Hylton, Chapter 5, Verse 17. Misa is the mother of Justin, Sean "P. Diddy" Comb's oldest child. Ms. Misa had the man, the baby and the money. But guess what? It didn't work out. Now did she hang around like Kim Porter did through his relationship with Jennifer Lopez just because she felt that she was entitled to this man because she had his children and because she rode out with him when he had nothing? She had his first child, was with him from the bottom, but she didn't hold that over his head or her own! She did what a real woman would do. She practiced self-discipline and honored herself more than a relationship with a man that obviously was ready to move on. She took care of herself, focused on her career, and started a new life. She knew her worth!

But this falls on deaf ears to the women of the FWC. These women are defined by the pretty picture and what other people think most times. They would rather live in hell inside and look good to everyone on the outside. Perhaps she feels as if no other man will be better than this particular man. The bottom line is these women don't believe in themselves. As Michelle Obama once stated when an interviewer asked her how it feels to be the First Lady she responded, "Barack is the president of the United States, but any man that I would have been with would have become the president." This means that Michelle Obama knows her self-worth and she recognizes that she brings plenty to the table as a woman. Any man she touched would have turned to gold! Now that's some confidence for your ass! But the women of the FWC lack that kind of faith and knowledge of self. It's over! Let him go! Give him his free! So what you invested so much time in this relationship? So what you were with him when he had nothing? So what you got kids? So what? If the man is showing you that he does not want to be there anymore, let his ass go! He was with you for a reason or a season. Move on, pick up the pieces of your life, and bust a move already! It is not your job to worry about your baby daddy or ex-husband. It is no longer your job to care about where he sleeps, what he's doing and who he is doing it with. If you have children, focus on them adjusting to life without daddy living in the house. Focus on a cordial relationship between you and him, so the two of you can raise your children in a positive environment. You're not hurting anybody but yourself by sucking his dick knowing he has a new girl. Smirking at her and making her feel inadequate like you did something deep by fucking her man only makes you look dumb! You went from being his main to being a cum stain. What's fly about that?

We come from a generation of "ride or die" chicks that sacrifice so much of ourselves to show these men that we are down for them even when they aren't down for us. We compete so hard to take a man from another woman or to make a man want us. Why not compete in other ways like making the best of your life, moving on, being great, being successful, being wonderful, and having a great life outside of that failed relationship? You would rather spend all your time making a man feel guilty for leaving you. What is that about?

Stop holding niggas hostage! You will find that sometimes, if you have the courage to let them go, nine times out of ten, they will come back to you, stronger and better. Men respect a strong woman that knows her worth and that is not afraid to let go. But, in the meantime, no matter the outcome, respect yourself enough to walk away from a situation that is clearly trying to walk away from you. Your story with him has ended, and just like in most stories, the main character gets killed off, so a new character can come in to bring life to the plot. Move on and become the new character in someone else's life!

Gem

"Let people do what they want to do and you will see what they rather do."

THE JOSELINE JUX
How the side bitch ends up taking over...

Main vs. Side Chicks. My, my, my! Honey, where do I start? Okay, I need you Main Chicks, Wives, Wifey's and Baby Mommas to listen up and hear me on this. When a man has a "side chick," that is a whole other level of infidelity. You have to put yourself in a man's shoes and think for a second. What on God's earth would make someone have an entire relationship on the side? Just think for a second. What could your mate possibly be lacking in your relationship or marriage that allows one to be in an entirely whole new relationship...on the side? Just think... now, you take those answers and figure out what would make your man be in an entirely new relationship. Before you start calling the side bitches all kinds of home wreckers, stop and think. You could be the one that possibly wrecked the home, causing your mate to step out and engage in a relationship with someone else. Or your man simply has fallen in love with someone else. Yes, this is possible, ladies! Let's face it. The term "side bitch" is used for lack of a better term. I know as the "main/wife, etc." you would like to think that all this side bitch is getting is hard dick and bubblegum... on the side because you were there first, and you're his main, and you got his kids and blah, blah, blah. This belief helps you sleep at night. But be real with yourself. You're so hurt because you know, deep in your heart, that this side chick that your man has been spending time with is getting something from your man that you're not. And your man is giving her a part of him that he has never been able to give to you. Understand that the woman on the side, the so-called side "bitch", does not get treated like she is on the side, nor does she hardly ever get treated like a bitch. Stop sitting around talking about Side Bitches and how they ain't shit, how they need to find their own man, and about how ratchet they are. All that shit talking is not going stop your man from getting his dick sucked outside of your relationship. Your man went out and found a new woman.... keep that in mind. Putting energy into hating on her is not the business. Keep in mind. She is with your man because he doesn't treat her like she is on the side, nor does he treat her like she's just some bitch. You better peep game.

Now, I'm not here to glorify the Side Bitch, I'm really just trying to paint a picture for you to understand the predicament you are in, not your man and not her, but you! And while there really isn't that much you can do to get rid of her, you should understand how she infiltrated your whole set. He could be tired of arguing with you about doing things that will make him happy. It could be how much sex you give him, how you keep the house, not cooking, partying too much. There could be several reasons that he has to justify why he's cheating on you. Or he could simply just not be in love with you anymore, and it's hard to walk out of a long-term relationship, a marriage, a whatever, so he keeps you at the house, but he is with another woman setting up a new life. It is your job to recognize the situation for what it is and base your decision to stay or go on that.

Understand. There is a difference between a shorty, jump-off, booty call, and a Side Bitch. Those are the females your man sleeps with here and there from time to time. But the Side Bitch. She's getting time, money and in most cases his heart. Side Bitches (if she's a real good one) often get more than the main. Why? Because the main bitch is so hung up on that title that she forgot how she got the title in the first place and got lazy. You do know that the title ain't shit if the story doesn't match, right? Your man knows that you're content with "the title," and, as long you have that, he knows you're going to sit your ass down somewhere and be great. Meanwhile, he's treating the Side Bitch better than you; taking her to dinner, to the club, shopping, and if he is real bold, he may even slide in a vacation or two. Even if he only spends limited time with the Side Bitch, you better know its quality time. They don't have any kids running around and screaming. They are not talking about bills, things that need repair, or any other boring shit. Every minute they spend together is all about being great! So you got the title, but she has him completely. She's hanging with his friends while you're home looking for him and wondering where he is and who he's with. Why is this? Because you forgot how to treat your man? You stopped caring? I don't know. Is it possible that you forgot that how you got him is how you have to keep him? He married you. Now, you're complacent, feeling like you don't have to do shit else. I got the ring, girl. Fuck all that lingerie, cooking everyday bullshit. Now your husband is eating take out four days a week, coming home to you laid across the couch with fried chicken crumbs around your mouth, watching some IQ dropping shit on the television.

Not Side Bitches, though! She makes sure that, whenever he comes around, she's looking good, feeling good, and they are always ready to please, and it doesn't have to be all about sex either. The side bitch likes your man, so it's effortless to please him; whereas, for you, loving your man became a job, a job that you resent, hate going to, and see no room for advancement in once you became a wife, so you stopped working. Side bitches always have some kind of plan to please the man when he comes through. But not main bitches! Side bitches don't really beef. They appreciate the time spent with him. Not main bitches! All the time in the world ain't enough time for a main bitch! Side Bitches do what they have to do to keep him coming back, and they don't say "No" to anything he asks. Not main bitches!

So say what you want about her, curse the side bitch out and call her every name in the book for fucking your man, but that side bitch done got you demoted from Wifey to Might Be. You might wanna take a page out of her book and apply it to the next relationship you're in because your man, husband whatever is as good as gone, chile. There is no coming back from your man loving someone else. While you were so busy riding the shit out of the title, she was riding the shit out of your man, lighting his blunts, and cooking him all kinds of dinners. The Side Bitch could care less about a title. Truth is, she really doesn't care about you either, so don't bother calling her with all that raspy shit.

Okay, so now that you have become victim of the "Joseline Jux," (We all know who Joseline from Love and Hip-Hop Atlanta is.) What do you do? How can you deprogram him? Here's the answer: You can't! The only way to get him back is if this Side Bitch dies because, as long as she wants him, she can have him. Bigger than that, your man wants her! You have to get that part through your head. Your... man... is with another... Woman! They are in a whole other relationship, and the truth is you have become the Side Bitch. You are the annoyance in their lives with your constant whining. It's so bad that your house is in disarray when the Side Bitch catches an attitude with him. She has him so stressed, he's home yelling at you. When you are in a relationship and you truly love your man, it's not about going above and beyond jumping through hoops, it's about being the kind of woman that he will find it hard to replace. I'm not saying it's right, but sometimes check yourself to make sure you're not the home wrecker that you're claiming the Side Bitch to be. From the beginning of the relationship until you don't want him anymore, you need to cater to your man and fuck him like you're a side bitch. Don't ever, for a second, get to thinking you're irreplaceable!

Gem

"Cheaper to Keep Him may be true, but at what cost to you?"

RAY CHARLES TO THE BULLSHIT

Here's the thing. I really don't like to give "power" to the thought that all men cheat. Unless you have dated "all men," you can't really claim that as a fact. Maybe all the men that you dated cheated on you, but you can't give life to that statement. Now, we do know that men cheat, but they don't cheat all the time. They may cheat in the beginning of the relationship before confirming their feelings and position, they may cheat at the end of the relationship when they aren't in it to win it anymore, and they may cheat in the middle of it when things are all good, and you're none the wiser because you're all in love, but, at some point, you have to believe that your man is being faithful. Now, you have some men that are disrespectful, habitual line steppers. They cheat constantly; they stay in the doghouse for violating. And you have women that accept that. Then, you have the men that hardly ever cheat; but every once in a while, they step out and get their dick wet by another woman, and wifey is none the wiser because this guy doesn't overdo it. And nine times out of ten, he's taking care of home so well that, even if you did find out about that one time, you're not leaving.

The first thing that a woman needs to understand about men is that the teaching of what they need to do, in order to become a faithful man, is most times at a woman's expense, you feel me? Meaning we endure all the heartache, cheating, etc. before they become faithful, real men and sometimes it's not even for us, the next woman winds up getting the prize. Now hear me out. We all know if a man is not ready to settle down, he will sleep with other women and he will appear insensitive to our needs. Sure, you'll have the title of "main chick," but at the end of the day he's not ready to lock himself down to just one woman. It's fucked up, but that's just how it is. This behavior will lead a woman to ask, "Well, why not be single then? Why do you have to cheat?" It's not that simple, and it's not how men operate. All men need a comfort zone. They need that one woman that is in their corner while they run amok. But the wild part about that is that they wind up hurting this woman that loves them so much and they eventually lose her. Often, it is the pain of losing "her" that will change him and teach him, which goes back to what I said earlier; a man maturing and becoming faithful is always at some woman's expense. It's not until the guilt of fucking over "the one" comes down on them so hard that they change.

Now some men are lucky enough to get a second chance with that woman, and some just gotta live with the fact that he did her wrong forever! It's a wrap! So what happens? They move on, and they are ever so faithful to the next woman, which leads the ex to wonder, "Why wasn't he this faithful to me? Why suddenly does he want to be a good man?" A woman has to know it has nothing to do with her and everything to do with this man's guilt... and timing.

The big question is why do some women deal with cheating? Why do most of us turn the other cheek? Well, allow me to keep it 100 with you. Most women deal with cheating because ... dare I say it? They understand men! Yes, this is true. They understand that men go through these changes. And although cheating is for weak-ass Negroes, and when I say Negroes that goes for all races, sometimes, this is what men go through in order to get to the other side, the right side, because they are feeling weak! Also, women deal with men cheating because let's be real, if she's with a man that has her financially comfortable, what woman is going to give that up to not only be single, but struggling, while the man that she knows will take care of his woman, is taking care of the next chick?

See, this thing here is bigger than Nino Brown. It's not always about "being a dumb bitch" for staying. Women are catty and competitive; we will not let our man go, even if we don't want his ass, just for the sake of not letting him comfortably be with another woman. A lot of the time, the woman doesn't even love the man anymore. She just deals with his shit. She begins to use him in a way that she feels used. So while he's out cheating with the next chick, she's not really giving a damn. She has her own agenda as to why she is staying with her cheating mate. I'm sure you can relate to one of these reasons below.

1.Financial Stability: Nobody wants to struggle. Women want bags and vacations, money to hang out with their friends, etc. but, if you leave him, you won't have that free money to live life comfortably. So how do chicks think? *"Make him take care of me ... rat bastard."* You don't ever have to be home. She will never call you for shit, but bet, when it's the first of the month, your phone will be blowing up off the hook. Rent's due!

2.Dem Babies: Nobody wants to be a single mother or break their kid's heart. Why John-John and Floatasia can't have mommy and daddy in the house? Especially when a female wants to step out, she can make sure daddy is in the house with the kids while she runs around being ratchet.

3.Old Bitch in the Club: At forty-something years old, hell, even in your upper thirties, you're done clubbing and boy chasing. Who the hell wants to be back on the dating scene at that age? Online at the club in your old-ass mink and liquid leggings "tryna bag suttin." Girl, please! You know you would rather be home in bed sucking on your man's cheating-ass balls.

4. Embarrassment: When your long-term relationship fails, you have to relive what happened to you over and over again, every time a friend or family member finds out and asks you. You'd rather not, so you play dead while he's out fucking the next chick.

5.Insecurity: Who's going to want me with three kids, two baby daddies, and all these damn bills? These new niggas ain't into paying bills. Let me tell you that much! So, yeah, keep your ass still and be great.

6.Silent Revenge: Some women stay, so they can give their man hell and make him feel guilty for what he is doing. What she doesn't know is that he doesn't care, so she's wasting her time? The more you bitch, the further away from this relationship he goes, so keep on bitchin', bitch!

7.Timing: If you're a smart you hang around for a hot second until you get on your feet. Then, you leave his ass high and dry.

8.Emotional Stability: When you have the man that knows you like no other, fucks you like no other, and you both know that you will be hard pressed to find another like him ... you stay. Period. Where you going, ho? You're gonna wind up cheating on your new man with your ex, so save us all the damn trouble and have a seat.

9.Pretty Picture: This fancy picture frame with no pictures in it. That's what you look like trying to save face. Everybody knows your relationship is over ... we know! So when you come around your peers frontin', it's despicable. So stop. We see you. We not sleep!

10.Ring the Alarm: You remember that song by Beyoncé? She was going off singing, "Ring the Alarm, I been through this too long and I'll be damned if I see another bitch on his arm!" Even if she doesn't want the man, she doesn't want another woman to have him and reap the benefits of all the hard work she believes that she put into trying to raise him. But what a woman needs to understand is that men don't really care much about any of that. When they are ready to go, they are gone.

Now, with all of these reasons, you choose to stay behind to spite this man understand that you could be blocking your blessings by remaining in a relationship with someone that you are staying with for the wrong reasons. Is it worth it? Or, in the words of T.I., "Is ya happy?"

Gem
"We all must suffer one of two pains in life - the pain of discipline or the pain of regret. The choice is yours!"

LIFE AFTER DEATH

The feeling of losing love is probably the worst feeling ever. It feels like death! It feels like something in you has died when the man that you love unconditionally, does not love you anymore. The person with whom you once couldn't sleep without has no problem and wants nothing more than to sleep in a bed without you. Whatever happened between the two of you led to the unraveling of his feelings, and one day he makes his mind up that he does not want to be with you anymore, so he starts to do a bunch of things to turn you off. Little by little, he begins to plan his escape, and you won't even know it. Every day, he will devote some of his time to make you hate him that much more, because a man will never be upfront and just end a relationship. He will do things to make you hate him, so that you can either end things first or become so sick of him that, when he does end it, you will be relieved. Pay attention to the signs, ladies.

First, it will start with him not coming home, always having something to do, not coming over as much and spending nights out. He will have an excuse every time he is supposed to see you. Or, when he does see you, he will always have an attitude, have "something on his mind," or not be in the mood. His interest in you will begin to dwindle. You will become frustrated, you will wonder what's wrong with him, and you will begin to feel that it's you. He will tell you it's not. Do not believe him. It is you. He does not want to be with you anymore, and the mere sight of you gives him an attitude. Your breathing, the whites of your eyes, and the way you chew annoys him.

Second, he's not going to want to do anything "couple-like" with you anymore either. All of that going out to dinner and doing relationship things will end. He is preparing for you to deal with the fact that it's going to be over soon. No more movie nights or going to visit one another's families. If it's your birthday or anniversary, he will be reluctant to take you out or buy you a gift.

Dinner will be quick, and the gift will be basic. No more cuddling at night. In fact, he's going to come in late and start "falling asleep on the couch." He's about to get low on you and doing "couples things" will only give you the false feeling of things being okay between the two of you. Many nights, you will get dressed up to go out just to get let down. He won't be picking you up or taking you to work that often, if at all anymore. I hope you weren't the type of chick to shit on your people when you got a man, because you're about to need them more than ever!

Third, you won't be able to contact him throughout the day like you used to unless you have children together. He'll start ignoring your calls and not returning your text messages. Any routines you had going on such as "doing breakfast on Sundays," or "partying together on Friday nights," is dead. Don't bother calling his mans and them asking if they've seen your "him." They no longer fuck with you like that anymore either. They are aware of the fact that their friend isn't into you like that anymore, so they will keep their distance as well. Do not make his boys uncomfortable by being a stalker.

Fourth, sometimes days will go by, and you will not hear from this man. The extremes some men will go through to show you he's trying to get out of this relationship is crazy. He will make sure that, when he does resurface, he's calling you while you're at work. Yes, work. He knows you can't go off on him from your desk, so he'll call you, then tell you he'll see you later, but you won't see him later. He is putting a distance between the two of you for his smooth exit. You will beef; you will cry; you will accuse him of many things, and you will be right, but he will not admit it. He is going to keep doing what he does, so that you will leave first. I don't know why they do this sucker shit either.

Fifth, with all of this distance and curving, quite naturally, you will not be getting the dick the way you used to anymore either. This is when shit gets real. Men are not like women, they can't go for months or weeks without sex unless they're locked up. So bet that, if he hasn't touched you in days, he's up in something else. His dick won't get hard for you as quick as it used to if it even gets hard at all. You know this, and that is why you are really hurting and really mad, which leads me to the next sign.

Sixth, if you live together, he will start spending nights out and coming up with excuses. When you kick him out of the house after an argument, he's not really mad. He's "fake mad" and happy that this has occurred. Trust me. He is not spending the night out at his "man's house." When you put him out, he did not fall asleep in his car. His battery did not die. He is fucking someone else. In fact, on top of him not feeling you anymore, this woman that he is sleeping with now has expedited his escape. He spends nights with her, courting her, getting to know her. He is on to the next, but first he has to get rid of you. The more his feelings intensify for her, the less you will see him, and the more you will see how much he doesn't give a fuck about saving your relationship. You will deal with the pain of spending many nights alone, calls being ignored, texts going unanswered. Do not be a dumb bitch. Do not make excuses for his behavior. Men rarely move on from a relationship without having something lined up. They are needier than women in every way. We just show our emotions more so than them.

You know what this is. You know exactly what is happening to you and your relationship. So before you start begging him, whining, crying, sliding down walls with a fifth of vodka in your hand playing Mary J. Blige records, be a woman about yours, be real about what is happening around you. You should be above anything that you have to chase. You know what it is when you get that feeling inside that lets you know your relationship is over. This man you know all so well has changed. He is not the same, and he did not change for the better. You know that feeling you get at night when you call him and he doesn't answer, or when you doze off without hearing from him. The pain is so intense that it wakes you up at four a.m. and prompts you to leave him wild, long-ass text messages complaining, slandering, beefing, being disrespectful, calling him every name in the book because you are hurting. But your pain means nothing to him right now. He's on his selfish shit. He has to move on away from you, and his actions will hurt you, but it's him or you... and he'll be damned if it's him. So what do you do at this point? The crazier and more desperate you act, the more ammo you are giving him to use against you. He is going to use this for the reason he is leaving you in the first place. You will now become all kinds of "crazy broads" to him.

Once he begins to disrespect the relationship, it's time for you to start your journey. He's going to come through in the midst of all of this to have sex with you. This is not because he wants to be with you still. It's just something men do because they are selfish. If you fall for this, what will eventually happen is that you will go from being his wifey to being his side bitch or jump off. And then you will be at your lowest, feeling like shit, so do not do that! No more pussy for him! Once he shows you what it is, believe him! He has made up his mind and moved on already. Don't go having no babies or doing no bullshit to keep him around. He's gone. Let him go! Hold on to your pride if nothing else.

And, when you do move on, contrary to what popular demand says, "The best way to get over someone is to get under another," don't do it. You need time to get your mind right. If you really loved this man, take some time to go through the pain, the drama, the whatever. Deal with your shit! Don't lay up under some next cat that can smell your vulnerability and doesn't give a damn about your hurt. He just wants to get some of that good pain & pity party pussy. You know when you're hurting, you fuck like you're trying to get that mortgage paid. It's all passionate and deep. That's because you are still yearning and wanting your ex, and nine times out of ten, you're going to fuck the new man like how you used to fuck your ex. Now does that new man deserve that?

Practice Self-Discipline, woman! Respect the Curve. You have to! You have to take some time for yourself, and please don't share so much with your friends. They will put all kinds of crazy thoughts into your head, making things worse than what it really is. Just deal with the information that you have in front of you, don't go digging and searching for extra shit. That will only cause more emotional damage to yourself than you're already dealing with. Focus on getting through it by taking the blame off you and simply understanding that people change, people fall out of love, and all of this shit is fair game.

There is life after death, love will find you again and again and again, but you have to be willing to receive it no matter how many times you lose it! As great as your relationship is or was, understand that no one is exempt from heartache. In the blink of an eye, shit can change, so stay woke and be ready to heal yourself and start over again. You cannot worry about what your friends will think, or what your parents are going to say, what people on the outside are going to do. You have to always focus on you. And others need to focus on their relationship and just be there for you, whatever it is you decide to do. Don't give the emotion of "shame" so much power over the decisions you make in life. Because, when you think you won't make it and can't live without him, one day you wake up all alive and vibrant without him. And you move on. It takes time to get over a real true love. Do just that and always, always, always live again.

Gem
"Sometimes you gotta lose to win again."

LOVE IS BLIND

For those of you who haven't read my novel Full Circle, which is based on my life as a survivor of domestic abuse, allow me to share a brief story with you as to who I am and the life I escaped. When I was seventeen years old, I fell in love with a boy who I believed I would spend the rest of my life with. He was charming. He wanted me all to himself. He did things for me and cared about things that other guys didn't, like who I hung out with, how I dressed, where I went, what I did and when I got there. He loved me so much that he even proposed to me with a four-karat solitaire diamond after eight months of dating! Can you imagine a young Brooklyn girl like me, who grew up in the projects, walking around with such a huge ring? It had to be love. He gave me overwhelming attention, more attention than I ever got from any man, even my father, so I stayed with that man for four years, even when he began abusing me. I didn't pay attention to the signs. I didn't realize that all those things that I believed to be love were just ways for him to control me, and, because of that, I almost lost my life on many occasions. I endured beatings to the point of unconsciousness, strangulation, slaps, kicks, punches, being spat on, stomped on, thrown out of moving cars, beat in front of his family and friends, totally humiliated. I was mentally, sexually, physically, and emotionally abused every day for 3 ½ out of the four years of that relationship. I can recall weighing about one hundred pounds...wet. I was so broken. So, so broken. My hair had fallen out from stress. My face was discolored from unhealed bruises and stress acne. I had bald spots from my hair after being pulled one too many times. I was zombified. I did not care. I was just a body filled with a sea of blue, purple, and black blotches. Sometimes, when I'd be out in the streets, I'd look into the eyes of strangers, praying that they could see my pain and steal me away from this monster that was killing me. I was afraid. I was scared, and I was petrified to leave. Wouldn't you be if you were awakened out of your sleep with a fist to your back, or if your man pulled out guns on you and threatened to kill you? I prayed. I cried. I wished. I hoped. I did everything but leave. I had no support, not the kind that you need to get out of a situation like that. I had no one there to support me and help me get out of that situation. Nobody came to my rescue. Nobody saved me, and I knew I had to save myself. And so after promising God one last time that when I left, I wouldn't come back. I crept out of the house with nothing. It didn't matter. I had everything to gain and nothing to lose. I was one of the blessed ones to be able to get out, soldier on, and reclaim my life, and so my gift to you is to return that love that I wish I would have gotten back then.... Support.

Though you may not agree with the circumstances of a loved one, your consistency in supporting him/her is essential. It takes less time to DIAL 911 than it does to dial a friend to gossip about another friend/loved one being abused. DOMESTIC VIOLENCE IS EVERYONE'S BUSINESS. It is a serious issue that is often swept under the table and ignored, and the age limit is getting younger and younger. I believe that Domestic Violence Awareness should be taught at home and in schools, so the younger generation can be aware of what is not love, what is not respect, and what is not to be tolerated. As a survivor of Domestic Violence, one who had never witnessed it a day in my life up until it happened to me, I have an opinion as to why African American women "seem" to suffer from DV more so than other races in the United States. Most of it starts with the breakdown, break-up, and separation of family, single parent homes, including unemployment, poor education, bad housing, drugs, liquor stores on every corner. Our total economic make up is designed for us to feel hopeless. African Americans, without a doubt, have to work harder than most just to keep our heads above water. That alone breeds frustration, incarceration, impatience, self-inflicting abuse, self-hate, and worthlessness amongst other negative emotions that can contribute to being abusive or being abused. In hindsight, I do believe that I stayed because I felt that, regardless of the abuse, when things were "good," he gave me a love that I had been searching for.

I, also, feel that African American women find it harder to leave abusive relationships than other races for some possible reasons such as having less options as far as moving on and finding a loving mate. Because of the lack of Good Black Me or let me say this, the MYTH that there are no good black men, a lot of African American women feel helpless. They feel as if they might as well stay where they are. After all, what's out there? Another reason is that African- American women aren't that quick to call the cops, due to the racial injustice in the criminal justice system. We aren't supposed to call the law on our brothers, even if it is to protect us. Are you kidding me? Also, African American women seem to be more embarrassed by seeking help in a shelter system than they would be by getting abused by a mate. And lastly, on average, the African American female has a lower income than others, so it can be a difficult task to relocate somewhere safe and away from their abuser, as most abusers do provide the female with a better living situation than she is accustomed to in some cases. Embarrassment is one of the main reasons why some women don't leave. We'd rather isolate yourselves and fake happiness.

When you are young and impressionable, you grow up emulating what you see, you live what you were given, and you go off into the world with that frame of mind, believing that it is right, even though, deep down inside, you know that it is wrong. When children lack love, guidance, and support in the things that they do, from the people who raise them, they often go out into the streets for that validation. Sometimes, they pick up drugs, alcohol, or promiscuity to get that attention or to numb the pain that they feel from the neglect they were forced to live with at home. More unfortunate are those who turn to violence as a way to cope. And just as they felt hopeless at one point, they prey on those who are just as hopeless. They find someone to victimize. This is when you see young teenage boys man handling girls or young girls talking reckless and not caring about themselves. They allow these "boys" to beat on them because that is the only attention they know. Be it good or bad, its attention, and it is what they crave. It starts as a teenager and escalates into adulthood. Before their young minds can mature, they already have poisoned one another into believing that they need to stick together, both of them feeling like outcasts. Or you have adult men that prey on younger girls, or grown women who are looking for validation, so they allow a man to control them mentally and emotionally. Whatever the starting point, all of these victims have one thing in common. They are looking for some kind of void to be filled. Nobody expects to be in an abusive relationship. Most abusers hide who they are until they get their victim where they want them emotionally. Then, slowly but surely, they manipulate the relationship by isolating their mate, controlling them, verbally and mentally abusing them, followed by emotional and, ultimately but not always, physical abuse. The abused doesn't want to be beaten, raped, threatened, harassed, and nine times out of ten, they aren't staying because they are in love; they are staying because they are in fear. If the person you love can treat you this way, there is no doubt that you should believe him when he says he will kill you if you try to leave. And no matter the reason for being with this man, no one deserves to be treated this way, and everyone deserves to have someone in their lives that cares enough to help.

If you know someone who is abusing a loved one or is being abused, get involved. Talk to them. Call the authorities whenever you deem necessary. Provide a haven for him or her, providing that you aren't putting yourself in harm's way. Be positive, encouraging, and thoughtful when dealing with the victim. Be honest and blunt and, most of all, consistent with your help. Most people just need to know that someone really cares. Feeling neglected is what got them in this situation in the first place. Domestic Violence is a two-way street. Many of us like to look at the victims and feel pity and shame. We want to help them get out of the situation and save them. But contrary to what you want to believe, say or do, the Abuser should receive that same attention. I don't believe that abusers are born. They are, in fact, made. They become this way over a period of time because of what they were taught, shown, or how they were treated as children. When an abuser is verbally abusive, nine times out of ten, it's because of how they were spoken to as a child. There is anger deep inside of them, and the only way to get it out is to put it off on another human being that feels just as weak as they once felt when they were getting abused. They see that weakness in their mate that they possess. With physical abuse, it's the same thing. What is learned is often taught. The cycle cannot end if we do not educate our abusers on themselves and their own behavior. Once we show them understanding of their behavior (not to be confused with acceptance), then they will feel that love that they are lacking which causes them to act out in this manner. Once they begin to love themselves, then and only then can they love others. So before we throw an abuser under the bus, let's try to understand and get them the help that I'm sure they desperately need. If you know someone that's abusive to their mate or even themselves, don't turn your back. Hand them a pamphlet or the number to the National Domestic Violence helpline. I guarantee you that individual wants to be helped just as much as the person he/she is victimizing. Let's stop Domestic Violence one step at a time.

Where do we start?

What steps can we take to abolish Domestic Violence? Where does it start? Why does it happen? My belief is that abusers are not born; they are made. From childhood, the environment they live in and the things they are subjected to and allowed to see and hear shape these abusive behaviors. If they are not corrected, the lack of affection toward your children, the disrespect of their needs, the mates you subject them to, the relationships you keep, or lack thereof will all contribute to your child's psyche. Children grow to be young adults, and, at this stage, they will emulate what they were taught. That seed that was planted in them as children will begin to grow. In some cases, that growing weed will die, and a young adult will go the opposite way of the negative. But, in more unfortunate cases, that weed will continue to grow and poison the minds and hearts of your young adults. These young adults that are allowed to watch violent movies with their parents are able to interact with every mate their parents bring around, able to lash out and not be corrected for their bad mannerisms. These children are treated unfairly and in a way that is not beneficial to them. If they aren't taught to be respectful adults, a vicious cycle will begin. We all know it as Domestic Violence. I urge parents to not be cruel to their children in the sense of neglect, insensitivity, and carelessness when bringing mates around. Young girls run out looking for attention; young boys grow up with a lack of respect for women, and, with so many single parent households, it is hard to keep up with your own children. But we have to try harder, and the time that we do get to spend with them, we have to make it count.

When little boys are growing, we must tell them to give up their seat for a woman, hold doors for ladies. Teach them to say please and thank you. We must teach them to be helpful around the house. We must hug our sons, tell them that they are great, and will grow to be great men. Encourage them to pick up a book before they pick up a ball or a mic. Teach them to respect their elders and to never ever put their hands on a woman or disrespect them in any way. And for our daughters, our poor daughters, we have to go extra hard because daddy isn't around to be the role model that these young girls need unfortunately. We have to show them how to carry themselves in the street, how to date, who to date. We have to teach them to see how a man's family treats him before considering being in a relationship with him. We have to teach them how a man is supposed to make them feel, what he should and should not do. We have to tell them that there is no exception to the rules when it comes to disrespect. We have to talk to them constantly about their self-worth, letting them know that they are beautiful. We have to provide all of the love and attention that a young girl needs to feel wonderful about herself, so she does not search for that attention in a man. In an effort to stop Domestic Violence before it starts, Don't Be Cruel to your children, or they will believe it is all that they are worth, and they won't stray far from that when getting into adult relationships. No matter how old they get, they will always be your children, and you wouldn't want to see someone abuse them. If you see signs of anger in your children that don't seem normal, take them to see a therapist and nip it in the butt immediately!

Our women seem to turn to homicide in most cases or even suicide before they seek the help that is readily available for them. I encourage anyone in an abusive relationship to seek help. Whether it's verbal, mental, physical, or sexual, seek help and LEAVE, and, if you have a loved one in an abusive situation, do your best to support them. Learn more about domestic violence and educate yourself before you judge someone for going through this.

National Domestic Violence Hotline: (800) 799-SAFE

Web Sites:

U.S. Department of Justice www.usdoj.gov/vawo/

American Bar Association www.abanet.org/domviol/home.html

Here is a list of books (including mine) that I found on a website that can help you cope and hopefully move on a from an abusive situation:

Ayana Ellis, Full Circle, 2010 Available on Amazon.com

Marian Betancourt, What to Do When Love Turns Violent, New York, NY: Harper Collins Publishers, Inc., 1997

Maria Hong, Family Abuse, A National Epidemic, Springfield, NJ: Enslow Publishers, Inc., 1997

Cynthia L. Mather, How Long Does It Hurt? San Francisco, CA: Jossey-Bass Publishers, 1994

Susan Murphy-Milano, Defending Our Lives, New York: An Anchor Book, published by Doubleday, 1996

A.E. Sadler, book editor, Family Violence, San Diego, CA: Greenhaven Press, Inc., 1996

Jan Berliner-Statman, The Battered Woman's Survival Guide, Dallas, TX: Taylor Publishing Company, 1995

Karin L. Swisher, book editor, Domestic Violence, San Diego, CA: Greenhaven Press, Inc., 1996

Karin L. Swisher and Carol Wekesser, book editors, Violence Against Women, San Diego, CA: Greenhaven Press, Inc., 1994

San Jose Mercury News, Wednesday, August 4, 1999, p. 3B

Gem

"What kinda love from a ni**a would black ya eye?"

ME O'CLOCK

Do you ever find yourself foggy headed, unable to concentrate, tired, and just cranky for no reason? Or perhaps you know the reasons why you're feeling so drained, aloof, blah, but you can't really seem to figure out how to turn OFF your ON switch. You're always doing "something." Working, looking, building, trying, running, praying, giving, needing, loving, hating, hurting, wondering, thinking.... And it seems impossible to just stop for a second and do nothing at all. After all, the world won't turn if you're not running on that hamster wheel to keep it going, right? Wrong!

Life will pass you by if you are so busy trying to make a living, that you forget to live. Happiness will elude you if you are going so hard trying to make others happy that you forget to bring happiness to yourself. Love will drain you if you're loving your mate harder than she or he is loving you in return. In order for love to work, it has to be reciprocated on the same level to avoid resentment. That same sentiment goes for chasing happiness, chasing dreams, etc. In all things that you do, sometimes the more you chase after it, the harder it seems to obtain, and you will find yourself unhappy after a while because you put so much effort into things without giving yourself a chance to breathe and to get something in return. It's like planting a seed and just sitting there day in and day out waiting for a leaf or bud to sprout from the ground. Or painting a room, touching the paint every three minutes to see if it is dry yet. Applying for a job and expecting to hear from the employer in ten minutes. It will drive you crazy. Sometimes, you have to step away from the things you put the most effort into, step back, and get a clearer view as to what is going on, what you're doing, and what it is you're really trying to achieve. Look at all the areas of your life through fresh eyes every once in a while, to get a better understanding of what you're doing and what needs to be done next. If possible, change your scenery and surroundings for a few days, at least once every two to three months. Take a break, a breather, and invest all of that energy into some "me time." It's time to tell that schedule your on to fuck off and set that watch to "Me O'clock." Find something other than your normal routine to do or saturate your thoughts with. Step away from it all for a week or so. Regroup, reinvent, and apply that new energy to what matters to you the most.

Tips on How to Set Your Watch to "Me O'clock"

• Spa Day: Everyone should invest in a Spa Day. Get the kinks worked out of you and just relax. Let it all go. Breathe and get rubbed down by a strong stranger that may be in the mood to give out a happy ending.

• Change your surroundings: When your life gets too routine, it is imperative that you find something else to do other than the usual. Book a hotel room, one with a good view. Order room service, relax for the weekend, and leave the laptop at home. Don't even tell anyone where you are. Just let your loved ones know that you're okay and be gone! Enjoy YOU!

• Day Off: Use those sick/vacation days randomly in the middle of the week just to break up the monotony of it all. Nothing like a day off on a bitch-ass Tuesday.

• Fall Back: Relationships can be stressful even if things are going right. Let your mate know you're tired and you need a moment to yourself and switch that dial to Me O'clock for about forty-eight to seventy-two hours if possible. Let go of the emotional aspect of your life for a few days.

• Drop It: Stop thinking so much. Relax, drink some tea and let it go. Whatever it is, just let it go for a while. You may find that, once you do, you don't even have any desire to allow certain thoughts to enter your mind again.

• Reevaluate your circle: Friends/People can drain and suck the energy right out of you. Be mindful of who you spend most of your time with and who you give most of your energy to. They may be a huge contributing factor to why you feel the way you do.

• Career Goals: They say never give up. But you just might have to switch gears if what you're working so hard, and it just isn't working.

Overall, don't invest more time than you should into anything or anyone that isn't beneficial to your overall happiness, wealth, and health. Sometimes, you have to make time for nothing other than yourself to figure out your next and best move. Every once in a while, the time should be set to Me O'clock on your watch. It's okay to be selfish more than once in a while. Remember that your body/mind is a machine. Don't overheat it causing it to break down. Keep your parts fresh!

Gem

"Put that woman first"

YOU DESERVE BETTER

You know what's crazy? When a woman goes off on a man, calling him all kinds of liars, dogs, ain't shit, dead beat, maggot ass bastards and you ask her, what happened? And she tells you, "he used me, he dogged me, he didn't really want to be with me, it was all about sex, he's fucking with a million other girls, I was so good to him, I was loyal to him, how could he do this to me?" You can't help but to feel bad for this poor woman. And you can't help but to be mad at that dog ass negro that broke her heart and betrayed her trust.

But there are two sides to every story and the side that most women don't want everybody to know is the real side, the man's side. The victim is going so hard to make everyone hate this man for what he has done to her, when in fact he hasn't done anything wrong at all. You see, most women don't want to listen to a man or believe him when he tells her, "I ain't shit, I'm no good for you, I'm not ready to settle down." He has to wind up showing her how "ain't shit" he is because women are hardheaded. Some women are so high strung with ego's so big that they truly believe that they can be the one to change this man's mind. He told you who he was and what he was about, why didn't you believe him?

And so because you like this dude so much and because you want to be with him or with anybody so damn bad, what do you do? You go against the grain. You go against everything that this man has honestly, openly, told you about himself because you are so self-absorbed you thought your love, your loyalty and no doubt about it your pussy would change him.

So then what happens? This man sees you all vulnerable and wanting him, willing to do anything to get him in your life. What man that you know can resist the scent of a woman's vulnerability? He told you he wasn't about shit and that alone is his security for when you want to call him out on being a dog. In the meantime, he's going to fuck you whenever you call him over, he's going to let you suck him off, cook him dinner, spend nights at his crib, answer the phone in your face when other bitches are calling, all that! And in the beginning that may be all fine and dandy, but as time goes on that shit is going to wear you out when you see that all the effort, time, patience, lust and love that you put into trying to get this man to be with you is not working. So that love slowly turns to resentment and soon after... hate.

Now you're so mad and so embarrassed but you can't tell your friends that he warned you in the beginning. You can't tell your friends that he told you out the gate that this shit wasn't going to go anywhere, you can't tell your friends that he planted the red flag in the middle of your forehead because you don't want to look like a dumb bitch for dealing with him anyway and on top of that doing the most to be with him, so what do you do? You bash this man and make it seem as if he did you dirty so that you can get pity points. But is it even worth the heartache that you have inflicted upon yourself?

Ladies, I can't stress this shit enough. You cannot change a man, I don't care if your pussy can sing the star spangled banner and hum the tune to Good Times and when you give him head he can see into the future. NOTHING on this earth will change a man other than himself when he is ready. So when he says something to you, LISTEN! When he tells you who he is? BELIEVE HIM and when he shows you who he is TRUST that he is showing you the truth. You can't get mad at a man for taking advantage of a woman that doesn't even love herself enough to walk away from a situation that she has been warned about that will be disastrous to her emotionally and mentally. These boys out here ain't playing. You see them acting an ass that's because he is one. If you care about him or like him that much be his friend, have him in your life the safe way. It is very possible that he can probably bring something better to your life outside of something romantic and one sided. And who knows, you can be friends turned lovers when the time is right.

There is no need or reason on God's green earth for anybody to be with somebody who tells them from the gate that they are no good! Wanting to be with them anyway is a clear indication of what you think of yourself and what your self-worth amounts to. You're worth more than a fistful of tears and years wasted on a man that doesn't want you in a meaningful way. The sooner you believe that for yourself the less pain and heartache you will inflict upon yourself. Don't just listen to these men when it benefits you, listen to them when they are telling you what they are about and believe what they show you! Don't be a Dumb Bitch!

Gem
"Never take it as a loss. You're either winning or learning."

ALL MY SINGLE LADIES!

With so much talk about how to get a man, how to keep a man, how to stop a man from dissing you, how to avoid heartache, how to move on.... can we talk about being happy without a man though?

Being in a relationship is nice, but being single is not the end of the world! I mean, sheesh! Why are so many of us so pressed to be in a relationship? You got chicks taking fake pictures of her and her "bae." Women lying about the status of a relationship between her and "him," so she won't appear lonely, I mean what is going on, is it that deep? What is this obsession with being in a relationship? Now sure when you find the right one, there is nothing that can compare to the feeling of euphoria you experience when that jones comes down on you, sweet baby Jesus! When you are in love with a man and he with you and the two of you are having hot, sweaty, nasty, gutter, dirty iron staircase sex all day and night...you watch the sun rise and shine on him. He stares in your eyes and kisses your forehead with so much passion, and you talk to one another fifteen times a day about the same shit. You know that it's real when you can be around one another doing absolutely nothing and not be bored or feel pressured to do anything at all. When you have a partner in life, it gives you something to look forward to every day. Don't you just love love?

What about when you're single, though? Do you still love love or nah? Are you mad, are you bitter, or are you out there living for the moment and enjoying being a single woman who has the ball in her court, and on a good night, two balls, hello! There is so much more to life than being some foolish man's wife or some dude's flavor of the month or some "man child's" girlfriend or some idiot's main bitch. The world becomes your canvas when you are single. You have the option to choose and dismiss who you like and don't like. It's like being self-employed! You can make your own hours, take clients when you feel like it, and make up the rules as you go along! When you're single, it is the perfect time to fix the errors of your ways, touch up the edges of your life, reinvent yourself into whoever you want to be, and go out and choose or be chosen by the best of the best because you are in control of you!

And when you're single, try not to be bitter, try not to downplay others that are in relationships, just do you! Everything doesn't have to be "fuck that ni**a" and "men ain't shit or girl I'm glad I'm not in a relationship," rubbing your single life in the face of others. So what your last man cheated? So what the other one left you for no reason? So what you found out another one had a baby on the side? So what? Cut your losses, grieve, and move on! But you can't walk around with this *fuck a man* attitude, and then wonder why you are single. But if you really choose to be single and you're truly happy being single then at the end of the day the last thing you need to be worrying about is ain't shit lovers from your past and ain't shit ni**as that you haven't even met yet! You'll poison your mind the entire time that you're single with the notion that there are no good men out there and that you are glad to be single. How about focusing on just being happy and single with the ability to elude ain't shit men by choosing better, taking your time, getting to know a brother, being friends, dating, and, more importantly, basking in the glow of being single, and just doing you! Don't cut all your hair off because you're tired of dealing with it and then talk shit about women with hair or having to do your hair. You don't have those issues anymore, so focus on what's present in your life, not what you used to have and wish you did and don't want.

Be single, be happy, travel, spend time with friends, go house hopping, go shopping, pick up some hobbies, or simply do nothing. Enjoy your own company and bask in the ambience of a wonderful you! You don't have to keep busy when you are single to avoid the reality of being alone. Being single is not a death sentence and it doesn't mean you are lonely and have to be miserable around the holidays or when you see "couples in love." It just means the one worthy of you just hasn't met your wonderful acquaintance as of yet! Besides, if you can't stand being by yourself or around yourself, how can you expect anyone to want to be around you, too?

Gem

"The same chicks that are constantly telling you, 'Girl, fuck that nigga,' are probably the same chicks that will "fuck that nigga" behind your back."
#StayWoke

WHEN IT'S PRECIOUS, PROTECT IT

Women talk too much, and that is no secret. We feel that, to prove our loyalty to our friends, we have to share every intimate detail of our lives, because, if we don't and our friend finds out, she is going to feel as if you hid something from her. Muthafuck all that! You don't owe your friends anything in regard to your relationship. You surely don't owe them a play by play of your relationship and what kind of progress or lack thereof you and your man are making. It's really none of your friend's business what goes on between you and your man. Your privacy should be respected! It doesn't matter how cool you are with your girls and how much you trust them; shut the fuck up and stop telling them everything.

When you start dating a man, and you run and tell your girls every damn thing, then this man becomes someone special to you, now all your girls will know how big his dick is, how great he eats your pussy, etc. And I'm not saying that your friends ain't shit, but God has a funny way of revealing people to us, and he does it in a way that opens our eyes so wide you can't even front like you don't see what's going on. So be discreet about what you share with your friends about your man, be it sexually or just personally. We go through things with our man and the last thing you want to hear is that friend of yours throwing it up in your face.

Everything is not meant to be told. Remember your mother used to tell you that? Don't go out there telling family business. The same rules apply to your relationship. There is no need to seek validation on Facebook, letting hundreds of strangers in on your most intimate feelings. There is no need to put your business out there in 140 characters on Twitter for strangers to comment on your life. There is just no need to bring your business to the forefront of anyone's life, other than you and your mate. Most issues can be addressed between you and your man without anyone having to know there's a riff, and, even if they do know there's a riff, so what? Couples fight everyday B! But some women just talk too damn much and they put too much faith in their girlfriends. Fuck that! Don't tell them anything! The older you get, the more you should know better than to take your personal business outside of the house. You can tell your friends everything without telling them anything at all. Sometimes, details aren't necessary when trying to receive moral support from your girls. Girlfriends have a way of taking their friends relationships on as their own, jumping in shit that doesn't concern them, now your man and your bestie don't get along because YOU don't know how to hold water. Respect your relationship, ladies, and respect your man. The womanly thing to do is to maintain your silence and handle your business between you and him should a situation arise. If you want to vent to the girls, do so, but be tactful about it. Another thing women need to understand about their "friends" is that some friends give advice based on what they are going through, not what you are going through, and, sadly, some women don't know how to be happy for you even when they're going through hard times. That person needs to work on themselves before they can be a real friend to anyone. Bottom line is...Shut the fuck up! And you won't have to worry about your business being spread or your friend's unwarranted opinions about your love life.

Gem

"The truth is sexy. Speak it, live it, be it, own it and most importantly...HANDLE IT!"

THE YAYA SISTERHOOD

In a world of backstabbing, jealous, finding out your friends aren't really your friends through subliminal bullshit on social media, heartache, competition, and disappointment, there is nothing more refreshing than having some sister girls in your life that can uplift you when you're down. These are women who won't judge you, females who will support your goals and help you conquer your fears. Because let's face it, as women, we tend to keep things to ourselves and away from our "friends" because we don't want to be judged or we don't want anyone to put a damper on our mission to be great. But do you know how unhealthy that is? Perhaps, in the past, you trusted some girlfriends with personal information, and they let you down by telling someone else or even worse throwing it in your face during an argument. OUCH! So you feel as if you can't trust women, you can't trust your friends, and you have to keep your life private or only reveal certain information.

Maybe you have some goals that sound foolish when you say them out loud. A friend in the past shot your idea down, didn't support you, and it deferred your dreams, made you feel hopeless and made you crawl into a shell, not wanting to share your passions with anyone else. In the midst of all that, you're heart gets broken, that guy did you dirty, and you can't even tell your friends because "they told you so."

These are not healthy friendships... The older women get, the less tolerance we have for drama, bullshit, petty confrontations, and temper tantrums from friends looking for attention. Life's experiences should allow us all to grow and learn from our mistakes, so we can become better women, so we may be better friends, sisters, lovers, daughters, mothers... and not to say that adult women are above drama, but our drama as thirty-plus year-old women should be quite different and not as stressful as it once was as twenty-year-olds. At a certain age, one of your goals in life should be to seek, keep, build, and cherish positive relationships with like-minded people.

Friends aren't necessarily women that you've known since you were five years old either. Throughout your career and travels you may encounter the energy of someone equally great or someone greater than yourself to even you out and vice versa. Embrace her! Great women are attracted to great women! Don't be the kind of woman who says, "I'm too old for new friends." Friends are the gift of life! And, even if that friendship doesn't last, love it for what it was and what it brought into your life at that time. No one says you have to hold on to something that's not working, but it's definitely a great experience, and there is no harm in meeting someone new and possibly learning something that will be beneficial to you! Women normally have two sets of friends — women she knows and women that help her grow.

Girlfriends make the world go round. Whether they live next door, or on an opposite coast or in today's world, you'll know women whom you never met, but they live in your inbox! Positive vibes, good energy, awesome advice, and encouraging words should always be welcomed from women who are on the same level as you emotionally, mentally, and spiritually. For those of you singing "no new friends," you have no idea the world that awaits you when you seek out people that you can learn from, people that come from a different time and place, and people that you can learn new things and visit new places because of! The combination of women all in search of the same inner peace, happiness, and trust, can only lead to great relationships, drunken road trips, and the best memories that girlfriends can share. You need other women in your life to grow, learn, share, express, cry and motivate you, and, if the women around you aren't doing that, then, perhaps, you should consider reevaluating yourself and them as well!

Welcome greatness into your life by way of awesome strangers who provide great energy that you can't help but to be sucked in by! I assure you that it will ultimately lead to some of the best friends you have ever encountered. Some of my greatest friends are women I met along my travels on-line and in the most random places! I wasn't looking for friends, but, when you're a good woman, good women are attracted to you, and great friendships are forged. I meet women wherever I go. I talk, I laugh, I live, I love, and whoever is not for me will not be of me, and, therefore, will not be around me. I don't make the call... the moon above does.... Meaning, all you have to do is provide positive thoughts, words, and energy, and the Universe will supply the rest. What you're giving is exactly what you're getting. Keep that in mind whenever you begin to question the authenticity of your friends.

Gem
"When you score,
act like you been in the end zone before."

WHO YOU WIT'?

How many of you women have taken the time to do research on the man you are dating? How many of you feel funny about asking a man personal question, even if it is beneficial to your safety and happiness? How many of you gave up the pussy without knowing where he lives and who he lives with? How many of you done sucked a dick but, in turn, feel afraid to ask him when the last time he got an HIV test was? How many of you are more concerned with coming off as nosy and what he will think of you if you inquire, more than you are concerned about your safety and health? How many of you feel as if you'd rather not know because you might get turned off from such a "good thing."

There is no such thing as asking too many questions. You have the right to ask a man anything you please! He won't like it, but he will respect you more for it. We are grown-ass people. It's not right for a man who is interested in you to only provide you with his street name or childhood name. The first thing you need to know about this man is his full name. As adults, introduce yourself with your government. You will almost certainly get his government in return. Now, if he doesn't provide a last name or even a real first name and offers his "street" name or whatever, he clearly has something to hide. He could be a fugitive, a pedophile, or some kind of whack job, or he could simply be married. Ask to see ID if you're really on your job. Know who you're sitting across the table from. Protect your neck, ladies! Once he gives you his name, excuse yourself to the rest room and go Google his ass. Find out who is sitting across from you cracking open crab legs all willy-nilly. Find his Facebook profile, see who his friends are, what he's about, go to Inmate Look-up, check the sex offender's registry, and see what's good with your "him." You should ask him where he lives, who he lives with, where he grew up, where's his family is from, what he does for a living, and how long he's been doing it, and what he was doing before that. This is a first date conversation which should determine if there will be a second date. You should not be smiling, batting your eyes, or doing anything if you don't even have the basic information on this man. So what he looks good and smells good? That doesn't mean a damn thing when you wind up in a large dumpster with your panties around your ankles. Don't think for one second Detectives Benson and Stabler will be around to save your ass. Ask questions and be provided with proof and the truth from day one, ladies!

Gem

"Anything After "BUT" is Bullshit."

BEING THE BOSS OF YOU

We spend way too much time making excuses when we can be making moves. The energy that it takes to complain over something that we cannot change will better serve you by going a different route, mapping out a different plan, aiming for something better and more beneficial for you! Life happens, relationships fail, jobs get lost, friends do dumb shit, every season we will find that our life is shifting and changing and the people we adore aren't down for us anymore, we outgrew them or they out grew you. We are going to break up with the man we thought was the best thing ever. Ugh, why couldn't he deal with those unruly baby mamas? We are going to get hurt by girlfriends that betrayed us. Can you believe she told "such and such" all my business? And these jobs, honey. Lord, have mercy! These jobs are going to start making us angry. Every day, it's a full-time job not to drown your boss in the water cooler. So what do we do? Complain every damn day about it or get up and do something about it? Your relationships, career, and friendships are three essential components of your life. What do we do when all of these things are in disarray and our world seems to be turned upside down? I tell you what you're not going to do! You cannot, under any circumstances, compromise your health and happiness for either. Be the boss of you!

When a company isn't doing too well, money is being lost, and employee morale is down. What does a boss do? She or he holds a meeting, takes inventory of what is wrong, and, in severe cases, the business gets shut down until it is ready to be up and running properly again. This is what you must do when your life is spiraling out of control. Never mind the consumers. They will be back because you have the goodness in you that people want! You are in high demand! So close up shop and take self-inventory! When either of these things aren't working right, it is okay to assess the situation and let go and walk away if that is the best decision... for you! You come first in all that you do, even as a parent. If you're not in your right mind, then how can you care for those who are dependent on you? You have to be in control of yourself, your life, your happiness, and your health. Don't allow anything to control your happiness and moods outside of you. You have to learn how to survive when things are taken from you. You can't let outside sources validate your happiness because, in this life, everything comes and goes. This has been going on your whole life, but you might not have even realized it.

You have to set some rules down in your own life and keep it between you and your God. Set your standards and lay out the blueprint of your life to keep things in check. Have your standards! It's okay to want more and not settle; it is entirely okay! I'll tell you what else. It's okay to walk away. It is okay to outgrow your friends. It is okay to outgrow a job or a man, and it is okay to walk away for you. Do you think someone would think twice about doing it to you? It is okay to not want to date "that man" if his lifestyle is not conducive to your happiness and well-being. It is okay to say no and not have to explain yourself because you are the boss of you! Have your standards with a side of happy!

Surround yourself with people that inspire you to be a flyer you. That's what bosses do, they employ mirror images of themselves, people who are motivated, positive, go getters, over achievers! Place yourself around folk that are doing the damn thing, people you can learn from, and, while you are soaring to higher heights, remember that there is someone surrounding themselves around your greatness because you are going places, so reach back and pull one up! Pay it forward! You work hard. You deserve to call the shots of your life in all areas. Don't let anybody guilt you into playing small so that they can feel big on your watch. No, honey. Never give up on your dreams. No matter how long it's been since you've seen progress. Understand that, as long as you feel it in your gut that you have more to give, then keep on giving! Cast that net out a little further into the waters and reel in some fish! It's out there for you! Surround your entire being with individuals that motivate you to keep going. You have to keep going, the minute you give up is when you fail. Keep going and don't listen to anyone that tells you that it's too late to do what you've set out to do.

Boss up! Write the checks and cash in on your happiness. You hire and fire the folks when they're not on their job and you put mofos on probation in your life as you see fit. Don't stress nothing, and don't let anything stress you. Let your breath be your soundtrack, and breathe easy, mama.

Gem

"Players only love you when they're playing."

KING OR CLOWN?

You hear a lot of women addressing their mate as their King. But what a man King Worthy? Are you calling him that for show? To boost his ego? Or is he worthy of that crown that you have placed on his head? What are some of the qualities that a man must possess that makes him "the one?" We start calling these men "our hubbies" before they even think about buying us a ring. We go all out for these men for the sake of love before he has even proven himself to us. We force our beliefs on these men and trap them into conforming to our needs out of guilt. Yes, we do. Is that why they resent us sometimes? Because, instead of having a conversation about what we expect from a relationship, we start planning weddings in our heads. We have babies. We offer them keys to our homes, believing our own hype, and making reservations for two all without communicating our wants verbally and getting a response in return. Inadvertently, this makes them feel forced to comply with our emotional demands.

Can we admit that we do play a small role in the demise of our relationships sometimes? Because we assume instead of communicating? We feel that, because of all the hard work we put in, all the things we've done and in all the ways that we have proven ourselves "worthy" that we deserve rings and things in return? But who asked you to go all out? Did you do it from the heart or to gain something in return? Now, you feel burned, used, and betrayed, but did you ever communicate with this man about what he wanted... from you? And did you get any kind of confirmation from him that he wanted the same things as you out of the relationship? And were your trains scheduled to arrive at the same time? Or did you reach "there" first, and now you're rushing him, skipping stops just so that he can get to where you are, because you feel like you shouldn't have to wait?

When in a relationship with someone, it needs to be established early on what the two of you are hoping to get out of this courtship. It is your job, ladies, to ask questions in the beginning, put it out there, and, if that man is unsure about what he wants and where he is going, it's not for you to stick around and hope, pray, and wish that he'll change. It is not for you to bust your ass and go into overdrive to make him want to change. He gave you your answer, and, with that, you need to move accordingly. But many of us stay, trying to make something more of what we have. When you have a man that doesn't want to be married, doesn't want children, and is complacent in his lifestyle, knowing that you want more, why stay? Why pursue? Why not go after the gold, the real King? Why try to turn a pauper into a prince? We have to stop settling because we are lonely or because "it's time." We have to stop getting married for the kids, for the money, or for the amount of time we been together. We definitely need to be honest when dating. If you know this man is not husband material, why bother if that's what you're hoping to get out of the relationship? What makes a man a King anyway? Why do you want him so badly? That's what you need to ask yourself before you get too serious with a man. It would behoove you to consider some of the following questions:

1. What kind of family does he come from, and in what way does his upbringing affect him as a man?

2. How long did his other relationships last? What kind of women did he deal with? And why did the breakup(s) happen? Is he officially broken up with his ex?

3. Does he have children? If so, how many? What's his relationship with them?

4. What kind of mother does he have? How do the women in his family view/treat him?

5. Does he have gainful employment?

6. Does he have a history of abuse?

7. Is he affectionate? Does he know how to communicate with you? How does he react to bad/negative situations?

8. Is he a good example of a man to have your child(ren) around?

9. Does he help your life? Is he conducive to your well-being and happiness? Does he encourage you to be great?

10. What kind of friends does he have? Are they single or married? Do they approve of and add positivity to your relationship?

11. Do you feel comfortable speaking about spirituality with him?

12. In what ways are you compatible with this man?

13. Is he a womanizer?

14. Is he lazy?

15. Does he value women?

16. Is he in tune with a woman's worth, emotions, etc.?

17. Are you giving more than you are receiving in this relationship?

18. Are you clear on where you stand?

19. Are you in lust or in love?

20. Do you see yourself with this man long term? Or is he just a temporary fix for your emotional needs right now. Are you being honest with yourself and him?

It takes more than good dick and a couple of dollars to keep a relationship going. Also, don't be so delusional, ladies! Stop creating these relationships in your head before you get to know this man for real, for real. It doesn't matter that you've been dating six months. You really have to build a friendship and go through some ups and downs with a person to see who they really are and how they deal with tough situations. It's not all dick and dinner dates. Will he be there for you through hard times, or will he bail? Just like men want a ride or die chick, we need a no doubt be there kind of man for when we go through our thing! And you never really know a person until shit gets real and you see their true character. So hold on to that crown, you might be dating a clown and find out that you don't want him that bad after all.

Gem
"A promise ain't nothing but comfort to a fool."

RUN BITCH RUN!

I know he is fine as all hell, he's got that "Shit" that draws you to him. He smells good, he talks a good one, he is charming, he makes you laugh, and the sex is off the chain but girl! You know damn well you don't need to be fooling with him. Something inside of you keeps telling you to leave him alone. Pay attention to that little bell that keeps going off whenever you're about to see him, whenever you think about him or whenever he leaves your presence. Something inside of you says, I shouldn't be fucking with this dude. Why do you ignore that feeling? That feeling is a life saver! Now I know sometimes when we are in love, or when we are lonely, or when we are simply feeling a guy, we don't want to hear about how good he "isn't" for us. Friends can't tell us anything about this man we are so called feeling or in love with. Mama can't pry us away even if she beats us with a Martin Luther King fan in church in front of the pastor. So before you get in too deep, here are some reasons you should run away as fast and as far as you can from this man:

1. Violent: If he shows any signs of abuse on any levels, be it verbally, cussing you out, calling you out your name, intimidating you, belittling you, etc., mentally, trying to hinder you from pursuing your dreams or being around your loved ones, playing mind games with you by trying to make you feel insecure, unbeautiful, unhappy etc., physically, bustin' that ass for wearing orange or for any reason at all, then you need to run far! That domestic violence is no joke, stay away from these crazy ass men looking for a punching bag and be careful, because some men aren't looking for love some are just looking for somebody to take to the gutter with them. You are not his way out, his counselor, his chew toy, none of that, run! A woman should never feel intimidated by her man. His job is to love you and protect you. Anything outside of that, you need to run bitch run!

2. He's Just Not That into You: If everything he does is based on sex, you need to rethink your role in this man's life. He may have a woman and you just might be the jump off. If every time he sees you, you end up with his dick in your mouth, you need to run fast honey. Don't become the predator's prey. If he never hangs around, you when you're on your cycle that is a clear indication of where you stand with him. You can't give him none, so he has no reason to be around you!

3. No Ambition: I get that we all fall on hard times, but at the end of the day, a man's living situation says a lot about how he handles money and responsibility. If he can't afford to pay his own way, then what do you expect him to bring to the table in your relationship? So if his grown ass is living at home with his mother or has roommates, then you need to reconsider taking this man seriously. He clearly can't afford to pay his own way or he's too lazy and cheap to make the necessary moves to live comfortably. Don't put yourself in a predicament where you wind up having to carry a ni**a.

4. Unfinished Business: If he is in the "it's not like that" phase of his relationship? Run bitch run! Nine times out of ten, he and his girl are going through hard times. And he will tell you all kinds of foul shit about her to make you believe he is unhappy with her. Then almost naturally, since you want to be with this man, you will attempt to do all the things his girl won't do or do all the things he claims his girl doesn't do shall I say, and then boom, now he has you and her. You have now become his monkey bar. Even if he was about to really leave "her," now that you're in the picture he's going to do the monkey bar on you. He'll hold on to her, then swing over to you, then when he has enough of you, he'll swing on back to her, without letting either of you go. He'll always have one hand on each of you. Sadly enough though, most men will swing right on back to the one that he's been with and leave you out in the cold. So to avoid this, let that man end his relationship before you step in. Don't be a dumb bitch.

5. His Balls and his Word: All a man has is his word and it is very important that he keeps it! As women, we need, crave, love, thrive and trust our men when they are consistent. We look up to our men to lead our hearts to safety and to keep our mind at ease. The only way that this can be accomplished is if his word is his bond. So if his story is always changing, promises are always broken, and things are always going "the other way?" You might want to reconsider wasting any more time on this man. You will forever live in uncertainty, confusion, stress and heartache dealing with a funny style cat like this one here.

6. Hi Hater: You're striving every day to do your best to get ahead in life. You work, you go to school, you're pursuing your dreams and every chance your man gets he's trying to convince you that your plan is a waste of time. He's always trying to lure you away from your goals or make plans for the two of you when he knows that you have obligations elsewhere that will benefit your future. Your man is a hater, dump him.

7. Baby Mamas: I don't want to judge, but if the man has more than 3 baby mamas, don't become the fourth! Clearly this man has a pattern of getting women pregnant and not staying in a relationship with them. You are no damn different, your pussy won't change him, the last three didn't! Strap up, don't be a dumb bitch!

8. Social Media Whore: I don't know about you ladies, but nothing turns me off more than to see a man on social media dogging women or talking heavy shit about his relationship. This man is nothing but an attention whore, looking for false security and love by strangers. How pathetic is that? And how pathetic is the woman that wants to be with this kind of man? Stay away from this sucker right here. He's the biggest sucker of them all, always talking shit about people, women in particular on social media and when he gets with you, you will be no different, trust me. Now take these words home and think them through or the next status he writes might be about you!

9. Self-Absorbed: A little cockiness is sexy but when you come across a man that is so arrogant, is too absorbed in his looks and getting compliments, selfish, and only cares about himself, don't try to change him. Leave him be with his mirror and his misery. Because anyone that is that self-absorbed is clearly self-loathing. *Food for Thought*

10. Gray Areas: If you're dating a guy whose time can't be accounted for one too many times, nine times out of ten he has something to hide from you. I mean an entire day can go by and he doesn't call, hours go by, and you can't reach him, a week will go by you haven't seen him, and when he does finally come around, his reason for missing in action doesn't fulfill your needs. You still feel a little uneasy and unsure of the answer he gave you, so you just have to deal with it because you have no proof. Naw fuck that. The proof is in his actions. You ever seen someone go to jail for a murder even though a body wasn't found? Circumstantial evidence is what you're dealing with here. He can be out there raping women or knocking off old folks for all you know. If he wants to move like a crook, then you should move like a ball and bounce! *Don't Be a Dumb Bitch!*

Gem

"You gotta know when to hold em, know when to fold em..."

"WHAT DO YOU DO
WHEN YOUR MAN IS UNTRUE?

When you're man cheats on you, there are a million things that go through your head. Why? Who is she? Does he love her? What did I do wrong? You feel like shit. Your whole world comes to a halt, like you literally stop breathing and living for a duration of time. How can you look at or lay with the man that you love after finding out he was with another? That vulnerable phase you go through while you're hurting is the most crucial period. How you really feel about him will surface at that moment. What you really think about your relationship will become evident and clear, and your ultimate decision will peak its way into your heart and thoughts. But, before you vent all of this to your man, you gotta hear what he has to say. You know him better than anyone, and you deserve an explanation. Once those questions are answered or not, you have to pick up the pieces and make a move. With most women, our decision to stay with our mate after he cheats is often based on the opinions of others, who no matter how much you have told them about your love life, really don't know the bond that you and your mate share. Though friends can be of help in finding some clarity when you're hurting, the ultimate next move should be your own and should be solely based on the foundation of your relationship, what you feel in your gut, and yes, the answers that your cheating ass man gives you. Not what your friends think. Not what your mama said. Not what anybody feels but you first, him second. Because, at the end of the day, this is between the two of you.

After getting all the details of the affair, the first question that you need to ask yourself is, "Is this relationship worth salvaging?" If you feel as if he had something more than just a fuck with this other woman, it may be kind of hard to forgive him and take him back. Some men have babies outside of the relationship, some men give you diseases, and some men actually fall in love and build a life with another woman. Do you stay once you find these things out? Does pride take over? Self-respect? Does love really conquer all? So you have to take the time to figure out if he is worth forgiving. How bad was the damage? How far did he go with this other woman? Your decision to take him back can't be based solely on your emotions. There is a bigger picture here. Men do all kinds of shit because, most of the time, they never really think of the consequences and, they sometimes just take advantage of a good thing. No matter how great that woman is they have at home they sometimes, somehow find a way to fuck up and do the dumbest things. But dare I say that all because your man cheats, it doesn't make him a bad person, just as much as forgiving him and taking him back doesn't make you a dumb bitch.

If you have a car and it breaks down on you five years after having used this car for everything, will you replace it with another? No, of course not. Because you know this car is reliable and has never fallen apart on you before. So what do you do? You take it to the shop, see what the hell is wrong, fix it, and keep it pushing. Now, if the car continues to break down on you, then you can say, "Okay, I can't trust this car to take me where I have to go. I need to get a new one." So when it comes to forgiving your cheating mate, there are so many things to take into consideration before you dump him for good. First of all, it's not that easy to walk away from love and I mean real religious spiritual love.

Now, before you say, "If he loved me, he wouldn't have cheat." let me school you on a man and his reason for cheating. It's hardly EVER because he doesn't love his woman anymore. When a man doesn't love his woman anymore, he's gone. He won't even play these kinds of cheating games with you. Falling out of love could be a reason, but, nine times out of ten, it's not the case. You love this man. You may or may not be married, simply living like married folks, have kids or not, and this man whom you love, who is good to you otherwise, has fucked up. I won't call it a mistake. He fucked up. He hurt you. He lost your trust. He has been communicating inappropriately with another woman, be it sexually, emotionally, whatever. It hurt you. What do you do? I say, if his bad outweighs his good, if he is a positive influence in your life, if his sudden case of insanity doesn't overshadow the kind of man that he really is, and his overall character is that of an outstanding mate, then forgive him. You don't throw away a brand-new pair of shoes because it has a scuff and people are pointing at the scuff and making remarks. What do you have to prove by throwing away those brand-new shoes when you know you really just wanted to take them to the shop. You clean them up and throw them back on like nothing. The same method should apply to your relationship. Patch up the problem, fix it, and move on. But if the shoes have holes, scuffs, a broken heel, and a peep toe that doesn't belong? There is no fixing it. Throw them out and get yourself a new pair. Now, you know the rules, once you forgive him, you forfeit your chance to pop shit and bringing up his infidelity over and over again. Forgiving him means that you are done with the situation and there is an understanding between the two of you why this happened and why it will never happen again. Do not wallow in self-pity and try to make him feel guilty for what he has done. If he truly loves you, trust me he feels like shit for what he has done to you. He's hurting just as much as you are. You aren't making things better by bashing him and making him feel like shit. Once you've accepted the situation, forgave, and took him back, it is time to start moving forward with your relationship and rebuilding what you have. Talk to your man, get honest answers from him, and say how you feel. Take time to heal but don't be all dramatic with making him wait before you take him back to prove a point to anybody! You know before he ever cheated on you that if he ever did, you would forgive him. When you love a man ye, you will forgive him so stop frontin.' You can post all that hot shit on Facebook, talk shit to your girlfriends and do whatever it is you can to deny yourself the act of forgiveness. But if his overall character outweighs an unwise decision, you will take him back. Yes you will! Stop lying to yourself. Just be solid in your approach to him when you let him know should he ever fuck up like this again, you will be gone. The first time? Okay, alright motherfucka. You got that one, barely. The second time? Now he's just taking advantage and hasn't learned anything from how he hurt you and how blessed he is to have received a second chance.

Another thing. Don't lose out on your relationship because your friends are calling you stupid. Those bitches probably go through worse shit than you and don't tell you but want to judge you. It's not just black and white when it comes to true love and a woman's heart. Forgive your man, work it out, and be great if you feel the relationship is worth salvaging, and I'm not talking about because of the kids or the years or anything outside of you and him and the feelings between you both. But before you get into a relationship with a man, finding out his patterns and habits with other women is a big help when it comes to how faithful he is in relationships and how long his relationships normally last. Lastly, every error your man makes doesn't have to be dictated to friends and family. If he's not whipping your ass or smoking up the rent money, keep your business to yourself and work that out between you and him. Outside influences need to stay they asses where? Outside.

Gem
"In order to win, somebody's gotta lose...Don't let it be you!"

FOR BAD BITCHES WHO CONSIDERED SHOE-A-CIDE

WHEN NINE WEST WASN'T ENOUGH

I'd like to address the self-proclaimed "bad bitches," the ones that idolize the women they see on television, the ones whose main concern is to attract "men" who are just as empty as they are. Women who are possessed by their possessions. The material things they own are all that they think that they are worth. You know who you are. You get ass injections to attract ballers. You wear pounds of makeup to hide or enhance. You wear club dresses to the supermarket. You're at every party and every function, doing everything you can to get the attention of a man. You spend your income tax return on designer clothes. You work two or three jobs as a stripper, bartender, and waitress just to have money to keep up with this image that you believe a real man wants from a woman instead of working two or three jobs to live better. You fly to All-Star weekend in hopes of snagging a better life. You worship the women on reality TV and you pound the pavements of industry parties until the lights come on all for the sake of a come up. Girl, you've been in everything but a coffin.

You are probably the same woman that feels as if you should give it up on the first date because he spent $100 on a dinner date with you, when, in reality, you need to add gratuity to that bill and tell him to fuck off. But you're not strong enough to do that, and why? I can't judge you. I don't know you, but you know why you do what you do. Let me let you in on a little secret:

Being a bad bitch holds no kind of weight. Being a bad bitch is only for the moment and a man worth a damn will never take you seriously and will never settle down with you and wouldn't even care if when they are done with you, that one of his man's hit it. They don't care about all the time and effort you put into trying to attract them. They don't care about bags and shoes and labels and costs. They don't care about material shit on their woman. This is from the mouths of the men that you are trying to attract. Yes, I did my homework. Please don't shoot the messenger. This is what the fellas are saying, not me.

You will never be in a successful relationship with a man worth a damn if your outer beauty is all that you have to offer. Real men don't care whether you have on Gucci or Hoochie. A grown man does not care about the labels on your clothes, and he damn sure doesn't want all that M.A.C gook on his 700-thread count pillowcases and shams. But this society that we live in now is so materialistic and the pressure to keep up with the Joneses and to be accepted at the cool table has gotten ridiculous! Women are hell bent on being accepted by these men that deal with your type of women in such a disposable manner and the sad part is you don't even care! Like, how much does your soul cost? You chicks are literally risking your life to enhance your body parts to get attention from these men and they don't care! The guys you're trying to attract are sitting back and clowning! This mentality and behavior makes you a basic bitch. Not the women you call basic because she isn't dressed in designer shit from head to toe, but you!

Do you like yourself? Are you happy with the time and commitment you dedicate to look a certain way to please strangers or men that you don't even know? Are you out there posing to get chosen, hoping someone will like what they see and then do what with you? Fuck you? Fuck with you? What is it that you're trying to gain? You got your pussy out, posing in doggy style on social media to attract strangers. I mean, damn, how serious is your need for attention? And what man worth a damn are you trying to attract acting like that? What would any man want with a female that is so insecure and needy for the attention of a million men that she would do some of the things that you do? It's just too much of an emotional burden for anyone to want to deal with. I'm personally sick of you hos on social media showing your snatch that ain't even snatched no more to the world. Like come on now. You gotta do better than that. Tuck in those chicken gizzards you call a pussy and get some class.

A real man is more so concerned about what you do for a living, where you're going in life, what kind of mother you are or will be, what your goals are, how you carry yourself, what kind of friends you surround yourself with, how you keep your house, etc. Boys judge you by the labels you wear. That's it. Ain't no more to it. Is that all you're worth? The choice is yours. You can be a dumb bitch, dating little boys and feeling good because he likes your Dolce & Gabbana blouse, or you could be dating a grown man that thinks highly of you and wants to put you up in a house. You decide. Have fun at the club tonight and don't forget to do it for the vine, I'm sure your future husband and kids will be proud.

Gem
"An Abundant Mind Brings Forth an Abundant Life."

GET YOUR INDEPENDENT ASS OUTTA HERE... QUESTION?

She got her own house. She got her own car. Work hard, two jobs. She's a bad broad. *twerks* Yes, honey, you got your own shit. Can't no man put you out of his house, take back his car keys or his credit cards. You better celebrate your independence, honey! You don't need nobody for shit! Nope. You are home changing light bulbs, banging nails in the wall, falling off ladders trying to paint, carrying groceries up five flights of stairs, putting tile down in the kitchen, rearranging furniture and at night? All those designer bags, shoes, and pay stubs keep you warm. You say that you don't have a man because you claim that men are intimidated by your success. Now did you ever stop to think that, perhaps, men aren't intimidated by you but irritated by you?

Be proud of what you have accomplished. Yes, you should be, especially in a time when most women are taking shortcuts by doing "other things" to get ahead. You should be proud of yourself for sticking to your goal and accomplishing all that you set out to accomplish. But I have a problem with you being so mean, nasty, and condescending to others. Why turn your nose up at someone else because they didn't accomplish the things that you did? Perhaps, it wasn't in his cards to get all those degrees that you have. Perhaps, he's successful in his own right, and he's happy with what he has so far. Perhaps he needs a good woman to motivate him to higher heights? Have you ever thought for one second that your success can be motivation for the man that you are in a relationship with? Hell, just meeting a man and having him become attracted to you because of what you have accomplished may motivate him to be greater, but you don't even give him a chance because he's not up to your standards, and you feel as if that gives you the right to be a nasty bitch? You probably don't even realize the energy that you give off to men that make them not want to fuck with you but just fuck you, and, with each dick you get that doesn't stick around, you become more and more stuck up and bitter. So you hide behind your "I don't need a man," rants. Sure you don't need one, but I bet you want one! I bet you want a man that likes you, wants to spend time with you, and makes you feel "not so independent." Admit that to yourself first and foremost. Own your shit! But you're chasing them all away with this Ms. Independent attitude Baby girl, he just wants to get to know you, not hire you, so why are you out to dinner with him reciting your resume? Just by talking to you and seeing how you carry yourself, he knows that you're educated and classy and, possibly, high maintenance. You don't have to shove your paperwork down a man's throat. Then, you get in a relationship with a man, and, every chance you get, you tell him he ain't shit. You tell him how you can do better than him. You don't know why you're with him. You remind him that you settled to be with him and that you can be with any man you want to, but you chose him. Why are you so mad at him? I mean, let's keep it real. Can you really do better than him? You look good on paper, but that's about it. Am I correct?

You emasculate a man because he isn't what you want in a man, yet you got in a relationship with him anyway, because as much as you claim to not need no man, "settling for someone that you believe is beneath you" proves otherwise. Right? So who has the real problem—you or him? Why are your successes a man's failure? What is the real issue, and what are you really looking for in a relationship? Love, or someone you can make feel like shit to make yourself feel superior? How many times do you think that you can call a man out of his name, kick him out of your bed, and make him sleep on the couch before he has had enough of your attitude and leaves you? When you put that man out of your house, do you really think he's going to sleep on his mother's couch? Or in his homeboy's guestroom? You better believe that it's only a matter of time before some other woman is opening her door for him to come sleep. And then there you go saying men ain't shit. You have a lot of men that sacrifice being called a sucker or a pussy because they won't knock your head off your shoulders for talking down on him, and you know what? He's doing the right thing. Why let anyone make you stoop to the level of violence and hate? And women like you get off on that. Why? It doesn't take a psychiatrist to understand that there is a deeper issue here, and it's you. It's the same as when a man abuses a woman. There is a weakness inside of him that allows him to think that it's okay to abuse a woman. Breaking a woman down makes him feel empowered. It's like when a man with money offers to help a woman but throws it back in her face. Where is the love in that? If you are such a strong, independent woman, why do you act so weak? Why do you stoop to such levels to hurt people? Why not find a man that is you're "equal," so you won't have to emasculate him or be aggravated because he is not as successful as you? Why do you keep finding men that you can belittle? Perhaps it is you that isn't good enough for him, and you're the one hiding your insecurities behind your successes.

Now what I want to say is "Check yourself, bitch. I bet you that pussy is as stink as your attitude," but that would be uncivilized. You obviously have some soul searching that you need to do. So instead, I'd like to offer you this…Let that hurt go, ma. Hurt people hurt people, and, if you continue to chase people away with this higher than thou attitude, you are going to find yourself alone for the rest of your life, even worse you are going to come across the wrong man, who is not having your disrespect, and sad to say he will lay hands on you. You don't deserve that. Be nicer. Get to know the man. He may not look as good as you do on paper, but he may have some other things to offer to balance your life out. Go on, honey. Take a chance! Stop being such a stuck up Bloop!

Gem

"Know your worth and spend yourself wisely."

HEAVY IS THE HEAD
WHO WEARS THE CROWN

Social media is the devil sometimes, isn't it? The foolishness that you can come across on any given day about these silly rules that these men come up with about how a woman should act or be in order to be good enough for them is just ridiculous. Every day, there is a blog or a meme created about why men cheat, why women ain't shit, why relationships don't last, what you have to do to keep him happy, what not to do, how to be the best side chick, how to get a girl to give you head on the first date. I mean, damn is it so hard to just know your role, play it well, and get the rewards and awards for it? It's not that complicated once you know your worth and what you will and won't accept.

Unfortunately, if you were born any time after 1977, chances are you believe that it is a woman's job to take care of everything to prove that she is superwoman and that she is worthy of even being looked upon by a man. Today's woman has to know how to do everything. She has to know how to cook and clean, heal you when you are sick, work and pay the bills, go half on the bill when you go out on a date, deal with a man's inability to grow up, and be faithful because "he is just a man, and it is in there nature to cheat," deal with his side bitch to prove what a real bitch you are, have a six pack, no cellulite, full edges, and a body count below 10 for the sake of his reputation.

First of all, as a woman in a relationship, your role is solely dependent upon the man you are with. If you are with a bitch-ass Negro with no goals, no money, no nothing, your job as an involved woman will be that much harder when it shouldn't have to be. The same men that make a woman feel as if she needs to be superwoman to please them are the same assholes who make it rain in the strip club but will tell his woman that they have to go half on the rent, the groceries and other bills. These basic Negroes need to be shot with shit and killed for stinking.

Your role as a woman is to be independent, so that you may have a sense of pride and identity, first and foremost, for yourself, secondly, for your relationship! How you carry yourself as a woman is not all about getting a man or impressing these dudes. It's all about you. You should always have your own...always! Being able to take care of yourself is an essential key to keeping a relationship healthy as well. That goes for your man, too. Nobody wants to have to pull the weight of a relationship on their own, feeling as if they have to take care of the other person. Nor should they have to constantly worry about how their mate is going to eat and buy their own damn tampons. If you don't have anything to offer, you have no business trying to bring that into a relationship. Taking care of yourself to relieve the pressure from your mate is one of the biggest contributions to your relationship. But, make no mistake about it, ladies. No matter what you have and how independent you are, it is not your job to take care of ANY MAN! You are nobody's ride or die. You are not his mama, and you are not his babysitter or his provider. Your job is to be a positive, motivating force in his life. It is a man's job to provide for and protect you, not the other way around.

The moment that a man decides that you are his woman and the two of you are in a confirmed relationship, these are the things that he has to do for you. It's his right and duty as your man to make you feel protected—mind, body, and soul. You should have no doubt in your heart and head that this man has your back, not just in the streets if he has to beat the breaks off somebody for causing you harm but financially, mentally, emotionally. You have every right to feel loved, safe, adored, cared for, and beautiful because of what he provides. Because let me say this, these men have been trippin'! My goodness, they really do think that they are at war with us! The hardest (acting) women are the softest, and men have just lost the patience to deal with this type of woman. They aren't willing to break down our walls to show how much they care, they straight up don't give a fuck, so where does that leave us? We have to get it back to where these men were taking care of us, courting us, loving us, RESPECTING US. We can't be at war with these men, we can't try to be like them, we can't act like them or think like them. We are ladies, women and we just embrace that in all that we do. You catch more bees with honey, you know the motto.

A man is to PROVIDE for you...

Such as a woman is to be "submissive" to her man to make him feel like a King. It is a man's job to provide for his woman to make her feel like a Queen. Again, these Twitter Ni**as have no idea what they're talking about. They call it tricking or call a man a "sucker for love" if he is good to his woman, but you have to be good to your woman, or you will not have one. If you go back and ask any OG how he keeps his woman, he will tell you, "Work hard, stabilize the home and heart, and be the umbrella that the woman and kids find shelter under... always. Stimulate her mind and make her feel safe, and don't forget to keep her pussy satisfied and pocketbook filled." You think Ruby Dee and Ossie Davis didn't go through drama? You think Martin didn't put Coretta through the bullshit? You think your grandparents been together all of this time because of just love? Sure, they loved one another, but there is a system set in place to keep a couple together through hard times. Love alone won't keep that house a home. We need some respect, character development, sacrifice, and commitment going on. The man of the house took care of everything back in the day. That was his insurance policy on keeping his woman and keeping granny safe and at home taking care of him.

Grandpa gambled up the rent money, drank too much again, made it home late for dinner one too many times because he was probably out with that clap having Jezebel from up the road. Oh, but grandpa was on time. He was home when he needed to be. He kept the mortgage payments up. He kept food in the fridge for his woman to cook. He fucked grandma right. Yes, he did. Your granny, too. He did all of the things that a man was supposed to do. Grandpa made himself HARD to replace. He made sure he was resourceful, reliable, and dependable. He proved himself King Worthy from the start and cemented his place in his woman's life. He knew his place as a man and as the man of the house. There was no calling grandpa a bitch-ass, a lame, a good for nothing son-of-a-bitch, a lookin' ass ni**a. No, ma'am. He may have pissed nana off but bet you she put a hot plate of food in front of him every night, because he was the man of the house, by his actions, and there was no denying that, and she respected him no matter what.

Now, when a man can't hold his throne down the way he should, it doesn't give a woman the right to emasculate him, but he damn sure doesn't have any business talking shit and acting all "big dick" about things. He better not turn around and ask his woman for $20 for a haircut or $50 to put gas in his car!

Naw, homie. It costs to be the boss, and prices are going up every day! Yes, a man's crown is an insurance policy on the relationship. Let's be real here! Even India Arie needs a man that's able to buy her some cocoa butter and head wraps. Come on now. A man's job is to have his own and be able to provide for his woman and his kids. Do not feel guilty or like you're being selfish for allowing a man to provide for you in a relationship. Note the emphasis on relationships. I'm not talking about hos tricking off to get a pair of shoes. I am talking about a man and woman in a committed relationship. Yes, he should make sure the bills are all paid. This is how a man is supposed to run his household. Now, while I do understand that times are hard and some men may not be financially capable of pulling this off, this is something you both should consider before moving IN with one another and/or having babies. Going half is cool, provided the fact that he's not spending his leftovers on some bullshit every month. Don't tell a woman you don't have the rent money then walk up in the house with two pairs of Jordan's and some new electronic gadget.

Know your role, ladies, and play it well. It is not your job to pull the cart while your man files his nails. It is his job to go out, hunt the food, kill it, and bring it home. Your job is to cook it and feed the family. You have nothing to prove, and you are with the wrong man if you feel the pressure of having to provide for him. If you are playing the role of the man, then what is your man doing? Taking it in the ass and walking around in lingerie? It is not your job to raise a man! His mama failed at it, and nana couldn't help either. What makes you think that you have magical answers? It is not your job! Ladies, I know that you feel as if we are in competition with these men, but we are not! Don't let these boys confuse you and your role. Don't just give yourself away and stamp "approved" on any man's forehead for the sake of saying you have a man. Meanwhile, you're going through hell behind closed doors because your man is really a slouch. Your job is not to give a man money or to buy or do shit for him. If he falls on hard times, encourage him to keep going, leave applications on his pillow and help him out. Sure, pray for his ass, but you can't coddle no grown-ass man and make him feel as if you are going to care for him. Fuck no! Even if your man falls on hard times and you bail him out here and there, limit what you give and how much you give. He has to want to get up off his ass every minute of the day to keep his spot on the throne. He has to be a man 24/7! A real man wouldn't even put his woman in a position to have to take care of him. There are a million hustles in the world, and he will go out and find one to continue to take care of his home. I don't know who raised you women that are out here taking care of these men financially, buying them all kinds of gifts and spending obscene amounts of money on him to "make him feel good." How can you allow a man to share your bed when he isn't sharing no bread?

Know your role, ladies and enjoy being all things woman. You deserve to be taken care of because you take care of yourself and your man. Let me add that when you do come across a man such as this, you better not take him for granted. Protect your relationship with the quiet fierceness of a lioness. Because quiet as it's kept, men like to feel protected, too.

Gem
"Put your faith in the man above your head,
not the man under you in bed."

MISSING OUT ON MR. RIGHT

Problem number one, ladies! You date for your girlfriends, don't you? Come on. Admit it. A small part of your decision to date any man that you've been with is based upon what your friends will think of him. You want someone that your girlfriends can be impressed by and slightly jealous of you for dating. Keep it real. I never understood dating a man to impress your friends. I mean, you have to be happy with that man not your friends! And then there are those of you that still want to try to turn a bad boy into a husband. Foolish child, haven't you learned that this will not work? There are some women that know good and damn well they have a good man, but what do they do? They mess it all up for a lesser kind. You have a man that wants to invest in a future with you, and you lose him by running behind some knucklehead that just wants to invest dick in you. Next thing you know, you're out with your girls talking about all men are dogs. With that mentality, you will never get a quality man because you're too busy fucking with niggas! Niggas and men are two different things. You want you a real nigga or a man? First, grow up. Second, Mr. Right probably won't be what you're used to, but let me ask you this, how has dealing with what "you're used to" been working out for you? You are so busy looking for this perfect man that you put together in your mind, but newsflash, you will not find the perfect man because you are not the perfect chick, despite what you may think! So the plan is to be with someone that can help you grow and you can provide the same for them. You can't keep doing the same thing over and over, dating the same kind of man and expect different results. It just doesn't work that way! Your type is not working out for you so learn from your mistakes, grow, and choose better mates. Don't let your pain be in vain.

Your energy and thoughts are your contributions to the world. In return, you will receive what you have been given. Allow the universe to pay you back for what you have contributed. Now if you're out there raising hell and being negative, what exactly do you think you're going to receive in return? You have to keep an abundant mind in order to live a life of abundance, if you are looking to change and to receive a different blessing. One of the things that you must do is distance yourself from women that have tainted views of men. These women that are often dogging men and talking negatively will affect your blessings. These women aren't in and have no knowledge on how to get into a successful relationship are not the women you should be congregating with and sharing your deepest, intimate thoughts with in regards to your love life. You have to grow up on your own and understand that not all men are deadbeats, all men aren't dogs. All men aren't out for just pussy... Okay, wait.... all men do want pussy, but some of them want more than that. All men are not out to hurt you. But, if you show that you are comfortable in your pain and that you don't want to be happy, half of the men you meet aren't going to want to help you out of that funk, they are going to treat you like shit because you treat yourself like shit. This ain't a movie. These men aren't going to save you. You have got to save yourself and want more for yourself before a quality man is going to even look your way!

Men show their feelings differently than us. Women tend to wear their hearts on their sleeves. We tend to let every man we meet know about the last one that did us dirty because deep down we want someone to save us and tell us that they won't hurt us in that way. There are plenty of hurt men walking around, looking to be saved as well, ladies. A lot of good men are out there praying for a Queen to come their way. But if we are walking around man bashing and taking their money without any regard or respect for them or ourselves, then what do we have? Most importantly, what do you stand to gain? We let a lot of men pass us by because they aren't our type, and don't get me wrong, you shouldn't compromise what you like. You know what turns you on, but some of us are ridiculous when it comes to choosing a "type." We will let a good man go because he wasn't tall enough, dark enough, wild enough, wealthy enough, and slim enough. Most likely, the man you need is not going to come in the package that you want. You are not going to get exactly what you want. He won't show up in the way you envisioned. Sometimes, you may catch feelings for someone uncomfortably quick, and guess what? You have to go with the flow. You just might be catching lightning in a bottle. But how will you know if you don't take a chance? There will be a flaw "according to your standards," and if you can deal with the flaw, then you can deal with it all. You know you're a good woman and that you have everything to offer a man. How would you feel if you were passed over because he thought you were too light skinned, your hair was too short, your chest was too flat, or something simple as that?

What about a man who expands your mind in order to comprehend life outside of the shit you're accustomed to? You can't keep wondering why you're single if you keep doing the same things. When it is all said and done, all of the bullshit we endured from these players in our past should have taught us something and matured us in ways to prepare us to be with our King, our Coach. You can't date soldiers all of your life. Be open to learning some things! Step into a different world and flow with the type of men who will show you something different outside of what you were raised to see! And another thing, what ever happened to being with a man and supporting his dreams? What ever happened to being a part of the plan, instead of wanting to jump in when it's all good? What happened to the support system? You will ride out for a man in jail, but you won't hold a man down that's trying to start his own business? You want to receive the fruits of his labor without lifting a damn hammer or a chair. You got nerve.

And then there is the issue of outside influences and constantly listening to what others have to say about your life. There comes a time when you have to listen to the voice inside of you and nobody else. You have to strike out on your own and be the only person held accountable for your actions. Your mother had a million failed relationships. You saw the men come and go while growing up. You heard the stories about how your father left her for another woman, and how men ain't shit. Any time you find a little bit of happiness your mother will convince you of how it's not going to last because men only want one thing. You have been hearing this for so long that you believe it. Every time a relationship fails, you say to yourself how your mother must be right. So you follow her lead. You treat men like they ain't shit and you give up on love. You don't allow yourself to be loved. You do not believe that you are worthy of being loved and that there is a man out there that simply wants a woman to love and that it is you. Some mothers will poison their daughter's minds to believe the hype. Your mother made some decisions that cost her a lifetime of happiness.

She made decisions based on how she was raised and her own life experiences. But your mother grew up in a different time and place. Your mother's mistakes are her own. You are not your mother. You are not her mistakes, and you were not there so you do not know why your mother is in the predicament that she is in. Perhaps your mother stayed bitter all of these years because she never grew up. Perhaps your mother had a type as well and never embraced change, never stepped out of her comfort zone and was too afraid to reach for the stars. Maybe your mother never learned to compromise her likes for her needs, so she remained lonely and emotionally stagnant all your life and hers. Maybe your mother's mother treated her the way she is trying to treat you, trying to instill negative values in you because that's all she knows. Mommy is not a bad person, but her life experiences has caused her to make certain decisions in her life... her life though, not yours! You never seen her smile, you never seen a man do anything for her, you never seen her in a relationship that was worth a damn. Understand that your mother could have made different choices, but she chose not to. She made her bed. That is not your burden to carry. You have the choice to show her how to do this, hon! Make her proud and show her what she's been missing and as long as mommy ain't dead she too has a shot at finding true love and happiness to last her all of her days!

And okay, daddy wasn't there. He left you heartbroken. That shit hurts, I know, I lived it! I wound up in abusive relationships, my mentality was fuck niggas for longer than I could stand, but there came a time when I had to stop abusing myself over someone that obviously didn't care enough about me to save me or prove to me that he loved me. I know that you were probably promiscuous through your teens and probably even in your adult life because your still searching for that love, you see hopeless when it comes to men because your father didn't set the example of how men should treat you and what you should and shouldn't allow. You made a lot of choices because of the pain that your father caused. You spent so many years hurting, looking for your father's love in all these men but at some point, you have to let go and stop using your absent parent as an excuse for your behavior. You have to come to terms with the fact that you are hurting yourself over someone that don't even know or sadly enough doesn't even care about the hell you're going through. It's a sad reality that most girls have to deal with but as women we don't have to live with "daddy wasn't there" syndrome. Grow up, get over that, and move on. If you love yourself, you will fight for your right to love and be loved in a way that you weren't loved as a child. You will fight for a better life by doing the opposite of what mommy did and attracting the opposite of what your father was. It's all about perception! BREAK THE CYCLE! You are no longer a child, let it go!

You want a King, but you still have a soldier mentality. But once you understand why and BELIEVE that you deserve better, you will change without even realizing it. You won't feel the desire to colonize with certain individuals. Yes, colonize. Like-minded folk have a way of creating a colony that makes their warped, miserable way of thinking normal. Once you realize that you are not of that, anymore, and that you can do better and that you want better, you will begin to do better and feel better about yourself, and a better type of man will be attracted to you, better people over all will be attracted to you! But it all comes with maturity and a willingness to let go of what was and embrace the life that you know in your heart that you deserve. You have to change. Most bad boys are notorious for never settling down, so what you don't want to do is spend a lifetime trying to make this man see that you're the one when you could be spending a lifetime with the man that already knows you're the one. We might play a game along the way with the players, but when it's time to be real, that's when you settle down with the coach and watch everyone else play the game. So don't lose a good thing over being too hard or too stubborn or stuck on your type. Give up some to get something in return.

When you're single for a long time, it's even harder to compromise because you're settled in your ways. But compromising doesn't necessarily mean giving up anything. It just means allowing someone into your life that can add goodness to it. After all, that is the only reason you should let anyone enter your space. If you're not benefiting from it, then it's benefiting from you, and how good can that be if you're not feeling the love? Our blood, sweat and tears put us into this corner where we are afraid to love again and all of the behaviors that I spoke of in this book are things that we do and accept while we are on this path to find not only ourselves but someone to love us for who we are no matter how much we try to deny it. At the end of the day we all want someone to love, and we all want someone to love us. We need love, yes, we do! And as much as we need to feel it, we need to give it! But you can't if you're caught up in the past or too afraid to make a change. Make all relationships worth your time. Make any and every man work for it. Make him show you how special you are to him! Don't settle for the bullshit because you're lonely or because you lack self-esteem, you deserve the best! Make some sacrifices and changes in your life and attract what's right and great for you. That life you daydream about every day is yours for the taking. Take the necessary steps to be a better woman and a better person. You deserve to have a good man in your life. You deserve to have good energy around you, and you deserve to be great. Don't ever think otherwise! Go get your blessing!

Gem

"Who Gon' Check You Boo?"

BE GREAT!

The world is so competitive, isn't it? For that job, for that spot, for that show, for those shoes on sale, you have to compete with so many other people that want the same thing that you want. And to top it all off you're a woman. What do you do now? When you feel as if you have to compete with anything or anybody, you've already lost. You don't have to keep up with anyone! Your lane is your lane, and what you do is all about you and nobody else. Your success is not measured by how much better you're doing than others, but by how good you are doing for yourself. Every day that you wake up and take another step to get closer to your goals, you win just a little more, and you become that much more successful. What you strive for in life is your personal affirmation.

Every day, privately, between you and yourself, work out the details of your life and do something, anything that will bring you closer to success. Whether you are trying to succeed in being happy, making more money, buying a home, letting go of negativity, forgiving, those goals should not be held up to a light against the world and what everyone else is striving for. Being great is not about being better than someone else, it's about being better than the person you were the day before. So before you stress yourself out by comparing yourself to the billions of people in the world, stressing over what they have, save yourself the mental anguish by simply concentrating on you, because other people have not walked in your shoes, and you don't share the same story, so how do you expect to share the same glory? Life is not about living for others. You have to live for you! Your main goal every day should be to make your tomorrows better than your yesterdays and always strive to be greater than you are today. And if you believe that you are already great, then strive to be greater! There is always room for improvement! Life is meant to be challenging, but don't think of it as hard work. Think of it as a maze with a prize at the end once you find the right path to take!

You can't go through life complaining and blaming others for your downfalls and hardships. We all have the same twenty-four hours in the day. Do better with your time! Do different things with your time! Change how you think. Change who you have around you. Change the way you live. Make changes to see different results. Own Your Shit! Stop blaming past heartaches, your deadbeat father and your neglectful mother on your current situation. The statute of limitations done ran out on blaming folks for your unhappiness! How do you look blaming someone else for your unhappiness? You are grown. Own your shit. You keep choosing to let these people have power over you, and what have they done to have power over you? Own your shit and keep it moving! One of the essential keys to happiness is to know how to move on when you're unhappy. What good are you to anybody, including yourself, in an unhappy, unproductive situation? Whose fault is it that you are there? Not your ex, not your mean-ass grandmother that raised you, not your mama, not your daddy and not that tired ass baby father of yours. Whoever you are, whatever you are, and all that you do is solely based upon choices you made. It is time to own your shit! The decisions you make in life are your own regardless of what input others may have had. Own that! Yes, that person hurt you, did you wrong, led you to believe it was one way when it was another, but when it was all said and done, you are the one that let them in, you are the on that let them stay way past their time and you are the one that ignored the signs. Now you're letting their actions consume you. Now, whose fault is that? Own your shit! You have to forgive yourself for what you have accepted in the past and forgive others for what they have done, so you can move on and live your life to its fullest potential. People are going to hurt you sweetie. The people you love the most, the people you thought you could trust, and the ones closest to you will be the culprits. This is a part of life. But you don't have to let it paralyze you and stop you from being happy. Accept it, acknowledge it, understand it, learn from it, let it go, and move on—in that order. It's time to keep living life and finding a better way of doing things, correct? Come on. Get up. Drop that dead weight off of you. It serves no purpose. Wake up. Snap out of it. It's time to be happy!

Nobody should have the power and permission to stunt your growth and thwart your happiness if you don't give it to them. People are going to be jealous, they are going to find clever ways to throw you off track, and they are going to want to keep you in a comfortable setting, so you won't grow. People are very clever in manipulating folks to not want to be great. You gotta be careful and mindful of those kinds of people. Folks on the bottom will always hate the ones on top. But you can't worry about that. You have to keep living and growing for you. It is not your fault that their ceiling is your floor. You feel me? You can't be afraid to tell these people to go away when they're trying to stunt your growth or make you feel guilty for winning and wanting more out of your life! You are in charge, and you are responsible for every emotion, every gift, every curse, every coming and going of every human being in your life. Stay in control of the wheel! Do not allow anybody to force you out of your lane. If you want a better life, speak what you seek into existence, live it, be it, give it, and you will get back everything and all the years that the locusts took. Condition yourself to choose Happiness over Hopelessness...

Woman to Woman:

Life is good! Appreciate each day and understand that it is God's way of giving you another chance to get it right. Take advantage of the opportunity you received today by waking up this morning and remedy whatever it is that you have going on in your life that isn't giving you joy. Don't give up on yourself! Give Praise! Respect yourself. Keep your pride and dignity in check. Never settle. Never place a price on yourself. Keep your standards real. Keep your heart pure. Keep your femininity in check. Educate yourself constantly. Take care of yourself and don't apologize for your independence. Love to learn. Own your shit. Stop blaming others. Don't judge. Keep your clothes on! Be a fiend for growth. Keep good folks around you. Teach what you learn. Find a reason to smile always. Keep laughter in your soul. Surround yourself with positivity. Forgive yourself. Keep giving until they can't get enough of you and keep God first in all that you do always! Before you seek your "him" try seeking HIM. Lastly, never dumb yourself down for anybody, make them smarten up for you!

Don't Be a Dumb Bitch!
BE GREAT!

Also by Ayana Ellis

Twerkin And The City
Don't Be A Dumb Bitch
Daughters

Watch for more at byayanaellis.com.

www.ingramcontent.com/pod-product-compliance
Lightning Source LLC
Chambersburg PA
CBHW031420150726
47989CB00002B/726